Untoreseen Impact

Ronnie Fox

Copyright © 2014 by Ronnie Fox
All rights reserved.

ISBN: 978-1-940449-06-7 (Paperback)

To Gwenn

Foreword

The story line of this novel is set in the gun-control debate that echoes across the news with every gun-related incident. The resulting clash of worldviews is real, and all sides are vigorously debated in the public realm. Few are able to truly ride the fence. Life experiences force most to choose a side, even if they never vocalize their point of view.

Unforeseen Impact weaves a tale through these emotionally charged waters. The characters are not real people, but their motivations are examples of the range of life-altering experiences with guns.

Fiction provides a glimpse into the author's imagination. Real places and events are seamlessly woven together with imaginary ones to create context and promote realism. Some descriptions of actual locations are necessarily adapted to fit the story. Any relationship to persons, living or dead, is purely coincidental.

Chapter 1

The mass of people was thick, and shoppers moved about at a slow pace, stopping to look as if they were truly interested in the merchandise at each vendor's display. Most would not purchase anything and simply move aimlessly about, following the general flow of the crowd. The smell of gun oil mixed with the sweet aroma of funnel cakes and the familiar smell of greasy fried foods hung in the air. There was an occasional whiff of sweaty body odor that assaulted the nose as the crowd made its way through the maze of tables filled with guns and gun-related merchandise.

The unhurried movement favored the vendors. Foot traffic was vital and a slow, steady flow of potential buyers is why they purchased table space at this show. The presence of major gun manufacturers, helped along by the lure of special gun show prices, drew more potential clients each year.

Clarke also counted on a crowd. He had researched the gun show market and had decided on this one for several strategic reasons. His top priority was to strike fear in the hearts of as many of "them" as possible. Therefore, the number of people he bloodied would multiply the impact.

The plan was simple; he would strike out at the gun-toting public on their turf. It would strike them right in the middle of one of their large gun-toting orgies. He would strike fear in their hearts and minds, even if only for a short time. Their fear would force them to face the truth and realize the destruction, and even death, guns propagate in society. He believed that some of his victims would experience such fear that they would never recover. This fear, he knew in his heart, would cause them to voluntarily abandon gun ownership.

Clarke had rehearsed the plan in his mind over and over again. In spite of his preparation, he now found that he had to work to control himself as his excitement grew. He was aware that his excitement was blended with a heavy dose of nervousness, but he had no idea how much the combination was actually affecting him. He tried to calm himself with the thought that he could not miss hitting numerous targets in a crowd this size.

He made his way through the service corridor to the catwalk access behind the stage. He climbed up and crawled out on the catwalk. The view was not perfect, but he could see the majority of the convention floor with only a few areas obscured by the hanging displays of the larger vendors. The lighting suspended on and around the catwalk discouraged anyone from looking his way. It did not make him invisible, but his perch, behind the bright lights, offered him virtual concealment from view from the convention floor.

The duffle bag he had rolled up in the panel of one of the backdrop curtains was still there. He slipped into his SWAT black paintball tactical vest. There were four refill canisters neatly arranged around the vest, each filled with 140 blood-red paintballs. The matte black vest served as camouflage in the shadows of the catwalk.

Clarke had shopped for hours online and had debated on a paintball gun that looked as much like an actual assault rifle as possible. The Alpha Black Tactical Edition with digital camo is designed to look like the M-16 tactical semi-automatic rifle issued by the U.S. Army. Yet, as he carefully planned each detail, he knew he could not risk the purchase of a new gun. It would be too easy to track. If someone were to see the gun well enough to think it were real, they would also have a good look at him. Most of all, the paintball hopper on top of any paintball gun is unmistakable. It simply changes the look, and especially the silhouette, of even the most realistic looking paintball gun.

He reached inside the duffle bag and drew out his weapon of choice. It was a simple, well used, paintball gun. He had purchased this one over a year before. He had bought two of them at a large open-air, community garage sale. He had made the decision quickly, paid cash, and left right away. The trail connecting him to the gun had long since dissipated. The gun would be left at the scene. It would provide no hindrance to his escape and no viable leads for the police.

The 200-round hopper fitted on the top was already filled to capacity. His repeated tests had proven that the freshly recharged CO_2 tank would be more than adequate to fire every paintball in the hopper and all of the refill canisters combined, several times over. The limiting factor would not be the number of paintballs; it would be how quickly he planned to depart.

A simple disguise was an elementary component in his escape plan. He could easily discard one or two articles of clothing and change his appearance completely. Escape routes had been carefully identified. Armed with the knowledge that even the best laid plans seldom work without at least some problems, he had identified several contingency plans. Even if he was blocked from the door that opened into the service corridor, he only had to reach the crowd. His first choice was to exit via the corridor, but he was confident that once he reached the panicked public, he would blend into the crowd and simply walk away.

The real risk was being pinned down on the catwalk. Since the stage area would not be used during this event, it was already closed to the public. That was something he had counted on and was one factor that would have forced him to abort had there been any last minute changes. He had also arranged a place to jump to at either end of the catwalk if necessary. The fact that foam rubber mats used for soundproofing were stored under the stage had made it easy. He had simply moved them to provide safe landing zones.

A quick escape was the primary way to mitigate the risk of being pinned down. His escape plan depended on doing as much damage as rapidly as possible and simply getting out promptly. The tactic was to strike swiftly and move on, allowing public panic to take over and do the real work.

Clarke scanned the crowd for the best target areas. He had ruled out the gun tables where the vendors would be facing his direction. He feared their experienced eyes. The area where food was sold offered an unobstructed target. It was generally crowded and was, without question, his first choice.

The second and third target areas, or kill zones as he preferred to think of them, were the long corridors that were directly in front of his position. The pedestrian traffic in these areas would provide an ample number of targets. They would be closely packed together and provide a high likelihood of panic.

Clarke breathed deeply. He had prepared carefully and reviewed his plans many times. Any delay now would only increase the chance of being discovered. He braced himself and lifted the gun.

The first rounds left the chamber with a familiar whoosh sound as each round was propelled by the compressed air. It seemed loud to Clarke, but he might as well have been using a gun with a sophisticated silencer. The constant roar of crowd noise was more than adequate to cover the sound of the paintball gun.

The first volley of paintballs was directed at the concession area. He had practiced firing the gun in rapid sets of three or four paintballs. This proved to be a very effective tactic.

The initial rounds landed on the backs of two victims. The sting of the projectiles caused both to lurch upward. One spewed Coke out of his mouth and all over those seated across the table. The other screamed as she rose, reaching for the stinging sensation on her back. The other patrons reacted to the blood-red blotches on their clothing, combined with the reactions of the first victims. Some began to panic at the sight of what they thought was blood.

One rather large man was struck in the back of the neck. The sting of the impact on bare skin was significant, and he instinctively grabbed the wound as he knelt down. However, it was the color of the liquid in his hand that caused him to yell, "I'm hit." He knew he was hurt and feared the worst. He continued to crawl to safety.

Similar scenes began to erupt around the food court. Some paintballs struck solid surfaces and splattered on everything nearby, including other customers. Other rounds impacted drink cups, spraying drink and ice mixed with red paint on those nearby. There were several other direct hits on people around the tables and others who were waiting in lines. Panic began to spread like wildfire. Screams of pain mixed with those of fear and panic. Some ran for safety, others crawled. The concession area was hurriedly being emptied in a mad rush of confusion.

Clarke worked hard to remain calm as he witnessed the ensuing reaction to the terror he was causing. However, adrenaline is extremely powerful and works not only to increase one's heart rate, it makes staying calm difficult for the most experienced and disciplined soldier. It was simply impossible for him to control his excitement, and it spiraled out of control.

The next rounds were aimed at the corridors filled with people in front of him. His aim was not as disciplined, but the effect was the same. The spray of blood-red paintballs landed on a variety of targets with the desired result.

A teenage boy was hit in the head by a volley of rounds fired in his direction. His bushy hair was greasy with paint that seemed like blood. He thought bullets fired into the crowd had hit him. He covered his head with his hands as he tried to escape.

Nearby, a woman was struck twice in the back as she sheltered her young son. She didn't know that the stinging sensation would only leave a bruise, so she feared the worst. Her mind wondered what her son's life would be like if she did not survive. She would have no regrets; her motherly instinct to shield her own child had taken control of her

Unforeseen Impact

actions. Others would never know the heroism of her actions.

Similar heroic acts played out in various places around the exhibit hall. Common people displayed courage in action as they sheltered others from harm. Some were protecting a family member; others protected complete strangers. In those moments when fear and danger met, there were more than a few that chose to risk their own lives to safeguard another. These selfless acts would not be recorded on any video, and for the most part, they would go unnoticed. Later, when the facts became clear and the apparent danger was correctly identified for what it was, these acts of heroism would be discounted and never thought about again.

There were vendors who were torn between protecting their lives and protecting their assets. Most found shelter under tables and made the most of a low profile. More than one had found his or her own firearm and was prepared to meet deadly force with an equally deadly force.

A few vendors had recognized the paintballs and were among the first to identify the hoax. Realizing the limited threat, they passed the word quickly among the other vendors. Despite the natural competition for market share at these events, most were friends with a tight bond forged over the years of working side-by-side. Their response was to band together.

In spite of the disarming word spreading among

the vendors, public alarm began to radiate from each of the three impact zones. Each zone produced similar results. The attack was having the desired effect. It did not take long to almost completely empty the entire exhibit area.

Clarke's perception of time was altered by the adrenaline coursing through his body. The vest was discarded quickly, with the refill canisters full and completely unused. The gun was hastily dropped beside the vest. The police would focus much of their attention on these items left behind, but they would not identify any solid leads from the used equipment. Their best lead would come from the paintballs themselves, but it would not yield anything substantial.

Quickly climbing down the scaffolding, Clarke slipped unnoticed through the emergency exit behind the stage. He removed the thin surgical gloves and tucked them in his pocket. There were others in the hallway, but they did not notice anything different or unusual about another person who appeared to be hurrying away from the danger just as they were. He blended into the crowd and disappeared into the parking lot. He had made his escape just as planned.

There were several patrons, mostly those experienced with paintball guns, who also correctly identified the projectiles as paintballs. They had little success calming the crowd once the panic began. In the end, the risk of injury from crowd panic posed the greatest danger.

The entire attack had lasted just over a minute. A total of 183 paintballs were discharged. They were delivered in short bursts, fired in rapid succession. The three impact zones had worked as planned and added to the confusion and fright.

Off-duty police officers hired from the local jurisdiction were present. They had been posted at the entrances and exits. They never had a chance to coordinate a move toward the shooter before he made his escape. Their initial response was to address the danger to the public, and their hands were full with the rush for the exits.

Amazingly, there were no serious injuries, although one barely avoided serious injury to his eye as a round glanced off his own nose. There were quite a few bruises, less than half were actually the result of the impact of a paintball. Most of the bruises and other minor injuries were the result of pushing and shoving at the exits. The stampede of humanity was to blame.

The aftermath of the ordeal was managed appropriately. The police responded quickly and identified the shooter's vantage point. The area was marked off with the usual yellow tape. Hours were invested in crime scene investigation. Yet, in the end, they would not find any leads that would bring them close to the shooter.

Chapter 2

Clarke watched the late night news with immense anticipation. He was thrilled with his work and wanted to see the panic and fear in their faces. He sought to celebrate his victory behind closed doors, where he could revel in his triumph. His attention to details in the planning had paid off, and he was enjoying his private celebration.

No one else had been involved; in fact, Clarke had not discussed any of his plans with a single soul. It was his plan and his alone. He had not done it for any credit. He didn't want any accolades. He was on his own crusade to change their minds about gun ownership.

The news team was the weekend crew. They relentlessly interviewed as many witnesses as possible. Jennifer, the lead reporter on the crew, knew what she was after. She wanted to advance her career, move out of this weekend assignment, and allow her talent to be demonstrated to a larger, more sophisticated audience.

She knew there had to be some great sound bites in the aftermath of this incident. She was more interested in capturing the tirade of a not-so-articulate bystander, than anyone else. Her motive was simple—to get her local news piece on the national circuit. She also knew that if her piece was going to get national attention, it would have a better chance if it reflected poorly on the gun show crowd.

Experience had been a good teacher. She had enough to recognize a good video opportunity. Gun shows would have those juicy bits of ranting about guns and gun ownership that would give her career a well-earned boost.

The crew found several willing candidates that were drawn like insects to a floodlight to the broadcast truck with its towering satellite dish. Jennifer's favorite was actually cut in the final edit. He had the perfect look, complete with overalls, a missing tooth and a greasy hat. However, he never spoke a coherent sentence while the camera was rolling. There were plenty of others that fit their purpose.

Jennifer asked her cameraman to capture footage of the sign because she would need a little more time than usual to explain what really goes on in a gun show. She was disappointed that most of the vendors had packed up so quickly. Her visions of low angle shots that panned across a sea of handguns were packed up along with the merchandise.

Her instructions to her crew were clear, "Get as much footage as possible. Focus on the loonies in the crowd. There's bound to be plenty of them at an event like this."

In their final version, the camera captures Jennifer standing in front of the lighted marquee sign with the words "Gun and Knife Show" as the background to the introduction. Jennifer began the piece with the simple facts that she knew her audience would want to know.

"Today a gunman opened fire on the crowded convention floor at this 'Gun Show.'" She chose to allow these words to briefly linger over the airwaves for effect.

"The name 'Gun Show' can be misleading to anyone who has never attended one of these events. It really is a flea market for gun dealers. Their advertisement boasts of 'thousands of new and used handguns' and 'thousands of new and used rifles and shotguns.' There are vendors here selling ammunition for the same guns that are for sale only a few feet away."

The background changed to a slow pan across the convention floor filled with police tape and crime scene markings. Investigators were visibly going about their duties.

It was no accident that Jennifer had allowed her intro about a "gunman opening fire on the crowded convention floor" to be separated from the fact that the gunman used a paintball gun. Although it was less than a minute, she knew the impact of those opening words. The power of a sound bite is undeniable. She finally stated, "The shooter fired a number of rounds from a paintball gun at the people gathered for this event."

The next segments were woven together from the crowd interviews. "Tell us what you saw," Jennifer asked as she thrust the microphone toward one of the bystanders.

"Well, it was crazy, you know. I thought there were bullets flying everywhere. I thought it was going to be a real wild shootout."

"How did you feel during this ordeal?" Jennifer asked another.

"I was scared to death. Never seen such a mess in all my days," a woman responded.

Her report continued and filled in the necessary details. The phrase used by the official representative of the police department, "No one was seriously injured," was not reported. In its place, Jennifer stated, "A number of the victims were transported to local hospitals."

To close out the report, the camera came to rest on the red paint that was splattered on one of the tables in the concession area. It was a great piece of camera work. The camera angle achieved its intent, and the paint gave the appearance of bloodstains. It served as the background for Jennifer's closing remarks.

She attempted to use her final seconds to present a pro-gun control point of view:

"Gun violence strikes once again. This tragedy represents the ongoing battle over guns in our society. These gun shows provide a major loophole in the federal law that requires background checks to be run for every gun purchase. Gun shows, like this one, do not require a background check for all firearm purchases. Transactions that are considered 'private sales' are exempt.

"A great debate rages over the Second Amendment. However, a much more dangerous issue is hidden behind the rhetoric. Some extremists support the Second Amendment because they believe it guarantees the right of citizens to rise up and over through the federal government, including armed conflict.

"It is events like this that cause many to question if guns should be privately owned at all.

"This is Jennifer Foster, reporting live from the scene."

Time constraints did not allow Jennifer to include more gun control propaganda. She threw her strongest punch in her closing statement and hoped for the best. She knew that the executives at the network level shared these opinions, and she wanted to get noticed.

As the video ended, the local news anchor read from the script of the teleprompter, "It looks like this was nothing but a hoax."

Her counterpart responded with a gentle laugh and then read his line, "Paintballs do pose a real danger, especially to unprotected eyes, but fortunately, this was only a prank."

After a brief pause, the broadcast continued.

"Hoax" and "prank" hit Clarke like a one-two punch. They not only took him by surprise, they stirred something deep inside.

For a moment, he was riding along on the wave of gun control rhetoric and enjoying the fact that his handiwork was being framed in the right context. He appreciated the fact that someone was articulating the fundamental elements of a position against gun ownership. But he was not prepared for the follow-up. His work was not a prank. He was deeply wounded when his actions were summarized as a hoax.

He had expected to see people still distraught with anxiety and was slightly disappointed that none of that had made the broadcast. But thanks to the remarks that were simply designed to transition to the next news story, Clarke was left with the feeling that the public seemed more amused than frightened.

Clarke played those words over and over in his mind. Each time he thought about them, his anger grew. The words fed a hungry animal that raged inside.

The local news anchor and her sidekick had no way of knowing what they had done.

Ray caught the report as he punched his way through the cable channels on his remote. He had been to numerous gun shows over the years, and he understood the setting very well. As he listened, he wondered how many in the crowd had left a loaded gun in their vehicle. He knew from personal experience that every major gun show in recent years prohibited anyone except police officers from carrying a loaded weapon. This gun show was one of the largest and was certainly carefully monitored. However, he also knew that those who frequent these events often own several guns and know how to use them.

He wondered how the shooter had managed to pull it off without being caught immediately. Most of all, he wondered if this person had any idea how dangerous of a stunt this was.

Ray turned off the TV. In his world, the paintball gunman was a fool. Ray replayed the story in his mind as he instinctively reached out and switched off the light. He quietly moved down the hall toward his bed, careful not to wake his wife. He silently slid between the sheets.

Sleep did not come immediately and his mind reviewed the news story as he laid still in the dark. He thought to himself, Someone should have told him not to bring a paintball gun to a gun show and start shooting at people. That's about the quickest way I know to get killed. He's lucky to be alive. His last thought as sleep finally overtook him was simple: There were probably more guns and ammunition in the cars and trucks parked at that event than in our town's National Guard Armory.

Chapter 3

Ray's eyes were open well before his bedside alarm sounded, one of the gifts that comes with an early routine during the week. He was usually up at 4:45 a.m. and out the door before 5:30 every morning for his commute to work. Lying in bed waiting on the alarm just seemed like such a waste, so he quietly got up and went in search of coffee.

The coffee maker had been prepared the evening before, a part of their daily routine. A flip of a switch and the coffee was brewing. It was not any special blend or an expensive brand name. It was simply the local store brand. Darla, their oldest daughter, had given him several of her favorite higher priced coffees as Christmas gifts over the years, but he always migrated back to the same cheap coffee. He drank it black.

Sunrise in these early days of December would not come until about 7:30 a.m. Ray sat silently on the porch and scanned the horizon for animals.

At first light, he would instinctively count the

cattle, a mental check of inventory. He was down to twenty-two head and was not sure they were worth the trouble. He paid someone else to do all the work now anyway. They were all in the fence close to the house until the end of deer hunting season. No need to have them out there where some trigger happy hunter might shoot one.

The air was brisk and the warmth from the coffee mug felt good. His thoughts tracked aimlessly in the darkness. Today was Sunday and Ray had agreed to go to church with Barbara, his wife, several weeks before, so he really didn't have a choice. He attended church once in a while, and he hoped his attendance today would count for the rest of the year. There were only a few weekends left in the year, but somehow he knew she would find another reason for him to go.

Barbara was up now and was busy in the kitchen. He decided he should go inside and see what she was up to. When he opened the door he startled her.

She looked up and ineffectively covered being startled by saying, "I was wondering when you were going to come in from the cold."

"I was just having my morning coffee," he played along. "What are you doing up so early?"

"We're having a potluck lunch at church today. I'm fixing to make a green bean casserole to take."

"Yes, I remember." Although he did not really

remember the lunch, he did remember his commitment to go to church.

"A missionary family from Africa will be there as the guest speakers, and lunch will give us all some time to visit with them."

"Sounds like fun," he added with a bit of sarcasm in his voice.

"Great!" she shot back, with equal sarcasm. "You will behave! I expect you to at least be nice to the missionaries."

"No problem, I'll be on my best behavior. I promise."

Barbara turned to the counter, signaling that the conversation was over. She went to work on the casserole. Ray recognized the signal and moved on. He was ready well before time to leave.

They arrived early and Barbara took her dish to the fellowship hall. Ray made his way toward the sanctuary. He greeted the other men and made small talk along the way.

He had been more regular in his church attendance when their girls were growing up. It was one of those things he did as a dad. Back in those days, he was even an adult counselor on a couple of student trips during their teenage years. He felt he had at least paid his dues as a church dad.

Ray was there often enough, and he had done his share of church duties, that most saw him as a good church member. But to Ray, church was just what good folks did on Sunday. He did enough to get by, and what he did at church, he did mostly because of the expectations of others. Ray had never had any deeply moving religious experience. He didn't really see himself as the type. He was a good man, and everyone would agree.

The church was a small country church with about a hundred people there most Sundays. All but a few were originally from the area, and everyone was known by his or her name and by the family he or she belonged to.

The service was designed to give the guest speakers as much time as possible. They were unusually good presenters for missionaries. They managed to keep it moving, and although they asked for money, it was done in a way that made it seem quite natural.

Lunch was like every lunch they had at the church, complete with Mrs. Nelson's yeast rolls. Everybody at the church loved her rolls and could not imagine a church-wide meal without them. Most of the women had "their dish" that they always brought. Ray had been to enough of these events to know what he wanted.

The missionaries enjoyed the opportunity to mingle and make personal contacts. The men began to gravitate to a table where they could talk. Ray decided to join them.

As he walked up, he heard David say something

about Smith and Wesson. At least this sounded like an interesting topic.

"The gun I use most is my varmint gun. It's handy around the farm," said old Mr. Latham.

"Dad, a 'varmint gun' is not a make of gun," said his oldest boy, Walter. "We're talking about who makes it, not what you use it for."

"Well," old Mr. Latham retorted with a smile, "you ask the older men around this table and I bet they don't care who makes it as long as it shoots straight."

"You got that right," said a younger man named Jeremy. "I want my gun to hit what I'm aim'n at. Don't matter much who makes it if you can't hit nothin." There was a gentle laugh from the group that showed their agreement.

Tommy spoke up next and said he liked Remington best for bird hunting. "They make an affordable and reliable shotgun. I've used the same one for years and have never had the first problem."

Walter cast his vote with a simple statement, "I think Smith and Wesson makes the best handgun for personal safety around the house. The M&P series are all easy to use. The M&P stands for 'military and police,' and they have earned it. They are perfect for stopping anybody who breaks in."

"You say that like you've shot several intruders,"

Brent said, half under his breath.

"Well, you know what I mean," Walter added in self-defense.

"I've got a collection of different makes of guns, and I'm not partial to any one gun maker," said Chris. "I don't think I care that much."

"I bet every man in this church has at least a half-dozen guns, and they probably are made by a variety of companies," challenged Doug.

"Most of 'em have a lot more than that," Jeremy said with a laugh. "I sure do."

Tommy asked, "Jeremy, how many guns do you have?"

"Well let me see," as he calculated in his head. "I'd have to think about it for a while. It must be around fifteen or twenty."

Ray began to take a mental inventory of the firearms he owned. He didn't know the total. He just didn't think about them that way.

The conversation continued, but Ray was caught up in the mental exercise of counting his guns. He started with his hunting rifles. There were three deer rifles—the one his parents gave him on his fourteenth birthday, the 30.06 he had picked up when he was nineteen and the one he uses now. Then there was a relatively new mussel loader he picked up from an old friend, two shotguns for bird hunting, a 410 that had been his dad's and a 12

Gage he uses on most bird hunting outings. His mind wandered to other rifles he owned—a 22 rifle that he had as a kid, accurate and reliable, and the old "elephant gun" that was his grandfather's, but nobody in the family really knew even what caliber it was or if it would even fire.

He began to mentally work on the number of handguns he had collected over the years. The starting point was the gun he used for personal protection and the reason he first got a license to carry a handgun. He had picked up the Glock 19 and kept it fully loaded. He had one extra magazine in the same holster. He kept it in his truck for his daily commute and beside his bed at night.

Ray had instinctively made his mental firearm inventory by categories of use. There was the occasional exception of those guns that he owned for reasons other than shooting. What he realized was that he usually thought of his guns in the context of their individual use. Those few exceptions were not used as firearms; they were collected for their uniqueness or some other special reason. To him, the most valuable one was not so because of its cash value; it was the pistol his father brought back from the war.

He was brought back to the conversation when someone changed the subject. Tommy asked, "Has anybody heard of the outfit down in Alabama that puts people's ashes in shotgun shells and rifle cartridges?"

Unforeseen Impact

"You got to be kidding," laughed Brent. "Who thought of that?"

"I'm not kidding," Tommy answered. "There's a website and everything. You can look it up yourself. It's called 'Holy Smoke' or something like that. I think it's myholysmoke.com."

"That decides it for me," Walter quipped. "Dad we're going to have you cremated and put your ashes in shotgun shells. We'll have the loudest funeral this county has ever seen."

"That's not funny," his father said, without even a hint of a smile. "You oughta respect your elders, boy."

"Dad, I don't mean no disrespect. I think it'd be a real honor. You would get a real dignified send off. Like a twenty-one-gun salute in the army, only more personal."

"This place really exists?" Chris responded with genuine interest. "I think it is a great idea. I wish I'd thought of it. I know a lot of folks that would be glad to pay for something like that."

The missionary approached their table. Everyone instinctively stopped talking, especially about guns.

"Oh, don't stop talking about guns on my account," the missionary offered. "I think this might be a lot more interesting. I've heard this missionary talk more times than I can count."

Ray smiled to himself. This guy was smarter than he gave him credit for. He just won the ear of every man around the table.

Chapter 4

Clarke arrived at the office building where he worked and parked in the same parking space he always used. He found comfort in the monotony of routine. His path across the parking lot, through the lobby, past the elevators, up the stairs to the third floor, to the right and then left into his cube was equally predictable. He was truly a creature of habit, and he liked it that way.

His duties were a combination of repetitive tasks that served as necessary, even vital, components in the back-up systems and routine maintenance of the company's computer networks. The monotony would be intolerable to some, but fit him perfectly. He enjoyed the isolation provided by his duties in the server room where he could escape from people for hours at a time.

But this was Monday and there was always a 2:00 p.m. team meeting on Mondays. Clarke viewed it as a necessary part of his week, but he still hated attending. He viewed the IT team members as either geeks or managers. The geeks actually understood the stuff the team did and, therefore, most of the topics on the agenda. The managers didn't know much about computers in general, but it never stopped them from trying to lead the discussion. Clarke tried to hide in plain sight in these weekly gatherings. He tried not to speak or get asked any questions, and he was usually successful.

Today's meeting was delayed in starting while everyone waited on the top-ranking manager to arrive. On these frequent occasions, the conversation usually bounced from topic to topic with little attention given to anything in particular. This was like any other Monday exchange, bounding aimlessly from subject to subject. There was talk about the movies seen over the weekend, the price of gas and whatever else was on anybody's mind. Then the topic hit a nerve.

"Did anybody hear about the nut that shot up the gun show with a paintball gun?" one of the lower ranking managers asked. "It happened not far from here."

Clarke tried not to move. He had been slumped down in his chair as usual, but he was taken totally by surprise. His mind began racing as if fire alarms were going off in his head.

"Yeah, nobody got hurt. It was just a practical joke or something," someone else offered.

Clarke was still reeling from the shock. He was not expecting the subject to come up. Yet, the reference to a practical joke hit him hard. He wanted to scream at the top of his lungs, "No, you idiots, it was not a practical joke! It was not a hoax or a prank. It was a demonstration of the horror that uncontrolled guns impose on our society!"

The topic quickly changed again when one of the geeks wanted to know, "Has anyone heard anything more about the new laptops we will be rolling out in the spring?" He paused briefly, "Will we get to have them ahead of time like the last time we rolled out new hardware?"

And that was it. The topic had changed for everyone except Clarke. His mind stayed glued to the paintball story. Once again he was stung by the reference to his work as a "practical joke."

Even though he managed to hide his reaction, he was glad the meeting didn't last long. He hid his emotions by remaining silent and worried that somehow someone might see through his shield.

The rest of the day Clarke managed to bury himself in his work in the solitude of the server room. The space was dedicated to racks of servers. It was relatively cooler than the rest of the work area and only accessible by those with proper ID cards and codes. He felt safe with the servers and hid there until it was time to go home.

Even though he immersed himself in his work, he could not escape the taunting words that flooded back into his mind — practical joke ... hoax ... prank. He was insulted. He was hurt. He was not prepared, and the loss of control made him intolerably uncomfortable.

He wanted to stand up and correct their complete lack of understanding. That's the problem. People like that just don't get it. Their stupidity and lack of concern propagate the mindless apathy that allows the carnage to continue. Guns will continue to kill and maim innocent, unsuspecting citizens, fostered by their own willingness to tolerate the loss of life and limb. It will only take a few that are bold enough to take a stand to change the tide.

Chapter 5

Kent Bree lived by the standards engrained in him from years of military service. His training served him well in both the military and civilian worlds.

He was always ready for the unexpected, and Helen was anything but what he expected. They were both at a party that neither really wanted to attend.

The party was one of many social gatherings in the early days of December that comes under the banner of a "Christmas Party," but has little to do with Christmas. It was just another excuse to throw a party.

He saw her from across the room and instinctively knew she was, like him, an unwilling participant in the festivities. He was not particularly good at pick-up lines and he would be the first to admit it. Knowing his own limitations, he simply walked across the room and introduced himself.

"Good evening, my name is Kent," he said with a smile. His intentions were simple; he wanted to pass some time until it would be safe to leave without offending the host.

She smiled back at him, "I'm Helen. Nice to meet you."

"I'm willing to bet that you came this evening for some reason other than to party."

"Is it that obvious? I certainly hope not," she glanced around as if someone else might have noticed.

"No, I just saw in your face the same thing I'm feeling. It was as if I were looking in a mirror," he wanted to keep the conversation going but was afraid he might have said the wrong thing.

"I'm here because I felt it was something I just needed to do for a friend."

"You must be a really good friend."

"What brought you here?" she was genuinely interested in finding out more about this guy. He's not bad looking, she thought to herself.

"I'm sorry to say that my reason is not so noble. I'm here because I thought it would be good for business since I was invited by a client," which was only partly true. He was invited by a client, but he came more because he didn't have anything better to do. Now that he was here, he regretted his decision.

"So, has it been good for business?"

"No, not in any measurable way. I haven't signed up any new clients or even connected with any good prospects," he answered honestly.

"So, what business are you in?" she gently probed.

"I'm a security consultant," he smiled again as he responded. "I am the founder and CEO of Bree Security Consulting."

She was pleased, although she had never actually heard of Bree Security Consulting. "Well I'm not sure what your company does, but I can assure you I'm not a prospective client."

"Well that's not why I walked over here." He was sure that the conversation was headed to an early end.

Helen, however, was intrigued and wanted to get to know him better, so she asked, "How does someone get into the security business?"

He was relieved that she had not responded with a conversation-ending response. "In my case, it was a natural next step after I retired from the Army. I spent most of my military career in security-related activities."

He began to be intrigued by her smile, so he asked, "What about you? What do you do?"

"I'm a high school teacher," she stated in a matter-of-fact tone.

"I admire anyone who will teach teenagers. I

couldn't do that."

"I teach math. Most of my students are juniors and seniors, headed for college. I actually teach AP classes in calculus and statistics, so I get to teach the best and the brightest."

"Is that the secret? Only deal with the smart, college-bound students?"

"It works for me. I've been doing it for a while now, and if you are going to teach in a public school like I do, students at this level are the most fun, by far."

They talked for over an hour, but the time passed quickly. It was evident to both of them that somewhere in the evening, their conversation became more than something they were doing to pass the time at a party.

Kent opened up and told her far more than he thought he would ever tell anyone in a first meeting. He surprised himself with his candor, especially about his two marriages that had both ended in divorce. He admitted that his years in Special Forces in the Army were bad for any marriage. What really caught him off guard were the feelings he began to have as the evening progressed.

She confided in him as if they had been friends for a long time. Her marriage had ended in divorce too, but she didn't give any reason. She just gave the facts and moved on to other, more pleasant, memories. The more they talked, the more she was attracted to him. She enjoyed the playful banter that characterized much of their conversation. She was having a good time.

Kent began to realize that the evening was almost gone. He kept looking for the right time to at least get her phone number or email. His own indecisiveness bothered him. He wanted to see her again, but he kept hesitating, partly because he was having a good time and partly because he just didn't want to take the risk of being rejected.

Perhaps she was tired, or maybe she just let her guard down for a moment, but what she did next was way out of character for her. She just blurted out, "Would you like to get together again sometime?"

There was no hesitation in his response, "Yes, I certainly would. How about dinner?"

"That would be perfect."

"Are you available next Friday? I know it's getting close to Christmas and there are always a lot of holiday commitments and other demands." He hoped his recovery was quick enough. He was afraid he sounded too eager.

"Friday would be fine."

"I'll make reservations somewhere nice and pick you up." He grinned when he said, "And I will need your phone number and an address."

They exchanged numbers and emails before he got her address. The evening had been much more than either had expected. What started out as a party that both were regretting had become the start of something interesting.

Chapter 6

Clarke was a man with a cause and was passionate enough to act on it, anxious to serve the greater good. He philosophically agreed with many serious proponents of gun control, yet he grew frustrated with the lack of progress. It seemed to him that the news still reported one act of gun violence after another, yet the carnage continued.

He never shared his thoughts with others. Not even with close friends. He really didn't have any close friends. He managed to keep others at a respectable distance. "Loner" was an accurate descriptor. He kept to himself and hid his thoughts from everyone.

The Internet was his primary connection to the outside world, yet he was guarded with even that liaison. His zeal for self-preservation and protection always outweighed his hunger for information. He searched cautiously for content that matched his ideals. He read far and wide, incessantly suspicious of every source. He diligently covered his tracks, using public computers at libraries for the lion's share of his research. Even there, he avoided any patterns that might create suspicion.

In his mind, he was looking for others who shared his convictions—guns are evil, and society would be safer and better off without them. In reality, he was fueling his own version of the truth.

Clarke used different search engines and a variety of methods to find articles that resonated with his beliefs. He read them over and over, memorizing much of the content. He saw himself in the text. At times he wondered if he might have written much of it himself in some parallel existence. His delusion was like a hallucination where his world became reality, his private world.

The articles, at least Clarke's reading of them, came together to form a carefully articulated thesis in favor of removing all guns from the public realm. They referenced several infamous shooting incidents and formulated an impenetrable foundation.

Outlawing and eliminating assault weapons and closing the gun show loophole were the first steps in his plan. For Clarke, the National Rifle Association (NRA) and others were the enemy. Each step along the way was a battle he was ready to wage.

Clarke had spent much of the day dwelling on the unexpected, stinging comments he had heard on the news and at work. Each was another unanticipated blow, and he felt especially betrayed by the comments at work. He had let his guard down, in what he thought was a safe place, and he was blindsided. He retreated to his apartment each evening after work. It was the only place where he was always in total control.

His apartment was neat and clean. The furniture was simple and obviously not where the owner invested his money. The computer and gaming equipment were where the money had been spent. He told himself that the latest gear kept him on the cutting edge, and he justified the expense as an investment in his career.

Solitude was his first line of defense. Isolation was his friend, and he enjoyed the protection it provided. Everything about his apartment was designed to isolate him from the world. Nothing, not even a pizza delivery, was allowed inside without careful examination.

During the afternoon, in the solitude of the server room refuge, he had begun to think more and more about those who shared his disdain for gun advocates. He decided he simply needed to look for his supporters and hear from them. So, he began to search the Internet for news and articles that told his story from his point-of-view. He had read many articles in the past and was certain there would be plenty more to read.

His initial query did find a few articles about his intervention at the gun show, but not the quantity he anticipated. As he read them, his disappointment grew. There was not much positive said about the event. In fact, most of the articles gave him and his attack very little credit as a serious act.

He checked the links to bloggers and articles on his preferred gun control websites. They weren't much help either. Some used the incident as a springboard to harp on gun shows in general. They blamed much of the proliferation of assault weapons, and gun ownership in general, on the easy access that gun shows provide. They leveraged every opportunity to restate their agenda. He never really found what he was looking for. No one seemed to understand his purpose, not even those who were supposed to be on his side.

Many news articles seemed to dismiss the event as a practical joke. This angered him more and more. With each degrading reference to his handiwork, his anger festered like a deep wound. The more he read, the less he seemed to find about his actions at the gun show. The hurt boiled under the surface. It wasn't obvious to him, yet it grew like a disease. Hidden somewhere down inside, the pain was drilling a hole. The vacuum it created began to consume everything around it. It was draining his energy and siphoning away his objectivity.

Clarke began to contemplate what it would take to truly capture people's attention. There must be a way to open their eyes to the truth, he thought to himself.

Although not really a conscious thought yet, Clarke

observed that people clearly pay attention when someone is gunned down. Killed or just wounded doesn't seem to matter. There is one simple fact, everyone notices when a gun or guns are used in violence and people end up injured or dead.

He couldn't help but notice that the mention of "Columbine" still evokes strong emotions even though the horrific event happened in April of 1999, well over ten years ago. "Virginia Tech" occurred in 2007 and left 32 dead. "Fort Hood" is remembered for the shooting there in November 2009. Early in 2011, near Tucson, Arizona, a U.S. Representative, Gabrielle Giffords, and eighteen others were the victims of gun violence. Six died that heartbreaking day. Giffords heroically lives on as a living reminder of the life-changing impact of a gun in the wrong hands. July of 2012 thrust Colorado into the headlines again as the "theater shooting" dominated the news. A few days later, another lone gunman killed six at a Sikh temple in Wisconsin before he took his own life after being wounded by police. A gunman at Sandy Hook Elementary School shocked the nation with the senseless murder of twenty young children and six adults.

Clarke had read about these tragic events and many others like them. He had studied them in detail. These events and other fatal shootings are still prominently mentioned in gun control articles and blogs. He wanted to make that kind of statement—one that would become a pronouncement of condemnation of guns.

He was fascinated by the fact that the perpetrators of these murders became infamous names associated with gun violence: Harris and Klebold, from Columbine; Cho, at Virginia Tech; Hasan, the shooter at Fort Hood, Texas; Loughner at Tucson; Holmes in Aurora, Colorado; Page in Milwaukee; and Lanza in Newtown, Connecticut.

He was glad he was not apprehended for his actions at the gun show, but he wondered what it would be like to become as well known as these. It never seemed inappropriate to him to think about these things. His were harmless thoughts that would never translate into action.

His search for support led to little comfort. It left him hanging. He felt that no one understood the genius of his tactics. The emptiness gnawed at him like termites silently destroying the framework of a house. Deep within, frustration slowly turned to hate and bitterness grew like a cancer.

Clarke's mind had become fertile ground for dangerous thoughts, the kind of mind games that lead to deadly outcomes.

Chapter 7

Kent arrived at Helen's condo right on time. He didn't often give much thought about what he would wear, but this occasion was somehow different. He was prepared to wait a while, but when she answered the door, she was obviously ready. All he had told her when he called with the details was the time he would arrive at her place and that a dress would be appropriate.

After considerable deliberation, she had decided to wear her long-sleeved red dress. It was a simple and classy choice. The neck of the dress came to a tasteful vee in the front, while the rest of the modest polyester fabric gathered to one side and then flowed into a flattering tea-length skirt. She determined this dress fit the description, the cold weather and the Christmas season. She accented the dress with a pair of black peep-toe pumps which added a good two inches to her height. In an effort to stay on the line between elegance and casual, she opted to leave her brown hair down, but curl the ends. To finish the outfit, she wore her favorite jewelry, a simple sterling silver heart necklace and earring set which her brother had given her.

This first official date made for a blend of excitement and anticipation. Helen had reviewed their meeting at the party. She had carefully replayed their conversation and searched her brain for every detail she could remember. She hoped her mind had not embellished the truth.

Her memory of him was framed by his personality. She remembered he looked like he was in good physical condition. However, what she really wanted to confirm was her impression of his gentle, but masculine, demeanor. She was interested in his looks, but his true nature and personality would require more time. She had enjoyed their first meeting and the depth of their initial conversation, yet she still had cautious moments as she thought about spending the evening with him.

Kent remembered she was good looking, but standing in the doorway was a stunningly beautiful woman. He thought to himself, They didn't make math teachers like this when I was in high school.

He walked her to his car. The weather had turned colder, adding to the traditional winter feel of the holidays. It also gave a practical reason for Kent to put his arm around his date any time they were outdoors. He was careful to gently shelter her from the cold wind without being too intimate.

He opened the passenger door of his BMW 528 as a

gentleman. Helen gracefully eased into the car and adjusted herself in the seat as he made his way to the driver's door. She did not know cars, but it didn't take an expert to know this was an expensive luxury sedan. She could smell the leather mixed with that unmistakable new car smell. The security consulting business must be lucrative, she thought.

They made small talk as he drove toward downtown. The weather was the first topic of conversation. It was a safe place to restart. They both agreed it was a beautiful evening; clear skies and the cold added to the spirit of the holiday season.

Kent wheeled into the valet parking area and the attendants opened both doors. They moved inside the building quickly, avoiding the cold wind that always seems to blow in between the tall buildings of any city.

Holiday decorations provided a warm welcome, and since Christmas Day was almost upon them, there was finally more of a holiday spirit in the air than just the decorations.

They made their way to the elevators. The Sun Dial Restaurant sits atop the Westin at Peachtree Plaza and boasts an unparalleled view of the Atlanta skyline. The three-story restaurant and bar rotates to offer a 360-degree view of the city.

As they exited the elevator and turned, Helen was impressed. The vista was spectacular. The city was dressed in her holiday best, and this vantage point gave an unparalleled perspective.

The view was a fitting backdrop for their conversation. Elegant surroundings and an intimate dining experience provided an ideal atmosphere for their shared plans, though hatched independently, to get to know each other better.

They checked their coats and were immediately escorted to their table next to the window. Each received a menu, and they both began to peruse their options. When drinks were offered, Helen order iced tea and Kent indicated he was fine with just water. They were seated facing each other, and their conversation naturally blended with their interaction with their servers.

Kent reinitiated the conversation with a question, "So, now that you are about to officially start your holiday break, how do you feel about having a couple of weeks away from your students?"

"It feels good. Don't get me wrong. I love my students. However, the lack of structure and routine for a couple of weeks will have a nice feel to it."

"I know what you mean," he agreed. "Vacation for me is mostly about getting away from my travel schedule and the routine of work."

"It will be a sweet reprieve from my normal routine, and I know I will enjoy the chance to sleep in for a few of the days. I won't miss the classroom and the demands that go along with it. The special thing about this break is the time I will spend with my sister and her family. I'll spend a few days with them at Christmas."

The server approached their table and offered appetizers. They both passed and opted for soup. They had decided on their choices for the main course, and the server nodded his approval as he made mental notes of their requests.

"Where does your sister live?" he asked, hoping it wouldn't be far.

"She lives in a quaint little town near Wichita, Kansas, called Cheney. She is a stay-at-home mom and her husband works in Wichita. She married a local guy from back home and they have stayed fairly close to where we're from."

"So you're from Kansas then." It sounded more like a question than a statement. He was disappointed that she was going to be so far away.

"Yes, I'm the classic farm girl that left the farm for the city. After college, I took a teaching job wherever my husband's job took us. The last place before our divorce was Atlanta. I stayed and he moved on." She didn't want to talk about her failed marriage, so she asked, "What about you? Where are you from?"

"I'm from here in Georgia, a town called Ellijay. It's about an hour north of here. It's a small town."

"I've been there," she remembered. "It was in the fall when the leaves were colorful. If I remember correctly, there are apple orchards in the area."

"That's home. My parents are gone now, but that's where I went to elementary and high school. I left there for college and never moved back."

She followed up quickly with another question, "Where did you live after college?"

"I joined the Army before I finished college and went right in the week after graduation. So I've lived all over the U.S. and traveled to some interesting places around the world. It was a great experience, and I made a career of it. I put in my twenty years and retired."

"What are your plans for the holidays?" she asked.

He looked at her eyes and responded, "I don't have any special plans." He didn't say all he was thinking, but he hoped that his plans could include Helen at some point.

Their soup arrived, and they continued to converse as they ate. They covered a variety of topics, including some things they had talked about during their first meeting. They were enjoying getting to know each other.

The main course was delivered next. Hers was the roasted chicken and his was the halibut. Each had perfectly carved vegetables designed to accent the flavor and provide a balanced presentation of color.

The food was excellent, but their minds were not primarily on the meal.

They continued to open up to one another, and the dialog flowed effortlessly along. The comfort level rose as the evening progressed.

At one point, Helen realized his experience and expertise probably made him a good liar. She wondered if things were moving too fast, yet she felt good about their relationship. He was a complete gentleman in every respect, even a bit old fashioned. She enjoyed the fact that he opened doors for her. He made her feel special, something she had not experienced in a long time, and it felt good, really good.

The food was delicious, and the evening was everything he had hoped. They both opted for a simple, light sherbet dessert. The only disappointment for Kent was that the time seemed to pass so quickly.

After dinner, he drove her back to her condo and walked her to the door. He had already decided that it had been a perfect evening, and he wanted to avoid any awkwardness about the evening continuing.

He preempted any potential uneasiness by saying, "Thank you for a wonderful evening. It's late. I hope we will have the opportunity to enjoy one another's company again soon."

She smiled and responded, "I look forward to it.

Thank you for dinner. It was delicious, and I thoroughly enjoyed the atmosphere. Most of all, I enjoyed spending time with you, and I look forward to the next time."

Chapter 8

News on the weekends seemed to be either everywhere or completely dead. Jennifer much preferred the busy ones. She thrived on the adrenaline rush and loved the fast pace. Running from one tragedy to another was what she enjoyed most about field reporting. Gathering information on the phone, doing some quick research and formulating a plan, all while the news truck raced to the next site was pure joy.

Weekends always had at least one sporting event, festival, cultural event or other community story that served as a backup remote assignment for her news crew. But, she preferred real news. The kind that allowed her to display her skill as a reporter and not just be a talking head on some meaningless assignment designed to fill a slot in the news cycle.

Slow news weekends, however, did provide time for research for an ambitious reporter like Jennifer. Quality research was always an asset in this business. Unfortunately, the timeline for most reports was incredibly short. One strategy for combating the rapid-fire nature of field reporting was to develop a backlog of information that could be spun into a story. She preferred to think of them as sound bites skillfully woven into first-rate reporting. Her laptop was her repository for these nuggets.

One benefit of her job was quality equipment. A reliable laptop with a fast mobile Internet connection had saved the day, or at least the news story, more times than she could count. Viewers would be surprised how much reporting is now based on a Google search.

Good field reporters master the art of making the most out of little. A quote from here, plus a slice of information from somewhere else, makes a reporter sound like a knowledgeable subject expert. Appearance is everything on TV. A news producer loves a quality field report, but authenticity, or at least the appearance of authenticity, is essential.

Jennifer, like any reporter, had her favorite subjects. Gun control was one of her passions. Her zeal was personally motivated, as well as professionally expedient. She operated based on her knowledge that the news executives at the network level were strong supporters of gun control. She was also aware that those behind the scenes, the people with real power and influence in the media market, always supported gun-limiting legislation. She wanted to show her knowledge and commitment to the cause.

On a personal note, she had been profoundly

impacted by one of her first real reporting experiences. A reporter's first look at a dead body is usually something that sticks with them for a long time. Jennifer's first was especially shocking. The image was forever seared onto the pages of her memory.

It was a tragic teenage death by a self-inflicted gunshot. The damage was extensive. At close range, the buckshot ripped a gaping hole in human flesh. The headshot was immediately fatal, and the results splattered on the wall behind where the teen had been seated.

Inexperience contributed to the shock of the horrible sight. She walked into the middle of the crime scene with a confident attitude fueled by ignorance and a total disregard for the ongoing investigation. She arrived shortly after the police and literally stumbled onto the bloody mess without any warning. The investigating officers didn't have a chance to shield her from the images that left an ugly scar on her memory and caused her to experience nightmares for months. Even years later, she struggled with the lingering images from the scene. It gave birth to a hatred for guns and set her on a lifelong mission to fight for the removal of all guns from society.

One small part of her quest was her file of gun control quotes and stats. She was careful not to overuse them, but she did manage to fit them in whenever she could. Guns were a common factor in many of the stories she covered. Drive-by gang violence, the seemingly endless string of homicides, and other firearms stories were all too common on her metro beat.

The news producer, Noreen, knew Jennifer harbored deep convictions against guns, but was unaware of the personal motivation. She leveraged Jennifer's emotion by giving her an assignment to prepare a three-part reportage highlighting the proliferation of firearms and the damage they inflicted on the communities in their viewing area. The timing was to coincide with the upcoming sweeps that would set the ad rate for the subsequent three months.

Jennifer welcomed the opportunity and began immediately to use every free moment to prepare. She scheduled several interviews to develop a collection of video clips.

One of the first was with a local police spokesperson. The police officer was articulate and all business. She was obviously comfortable with this type of encounter with the press. Jennifer asked direct, but leading questions. Her goal was to facilitate the use of facts in the responses. The experienced officer was well prepared.

The interview included a particularly useful nugget, as the officer responded to an inquiry about local gun shows and the "gun show loophole." She said:

"The Gun Control Act of 1968 governs the sale of firearms in the U.S. It is a federal law that requires businesses that sell guns to have a Federal Firearms

Unforeseen Impact

License and requires all guns sold under that license to be registered.

"However, guns sold at gun shows are often exempt from these requirements because they are considered a 'private sale.' A background check is not required for a private sale and that fact is often referred to as 'the gun show loophole.'

"Nationwide, there are more than 5,000 of these gun shows each year. These events include guns, gun parts, ammunition, gun accessories and literature. New and used handguns, semi-automatic assault weapons, shotguns, rifles and even historic firearms are bought, sold or traded."

Maybe it was the uniform, or the clarity of her statements, either way, the video was just what Jennifer wanted. She would later add her own gun show references like "uncontrolled flea markets of devastation" to make her point.

Jennifer yearned for the day when guns would be outlawed. Convinced that gun shows posed an emanate threat, she waged a private war to put an end to these events.

Another interview focused on "gun death stats." The interview was retrieved from video stored at the station. Jennifer remembered the clip that was not included in the previous report. It was a haunting reminder of her first experience with death by a gun. She retrieved the file and reviewed it.

An unidentified talking head stated many facts. Jennifer selected one: "In 2010 there were approximately 13,000 murders and most were committed with a firearm. Of the offenders for whom gender was known, 90.3 percent were males."

Other facts were given, but this portion suited her objective. In her mind, firearms are responsible for most murders. She reserved the video for her exclusive use.

She would research stats and stories on suicide deaths by guns, pro-gun control websites like the "Brady Campaign," gun control policies such as the proposed limits on assault weapons, quotes from gun control advocates in Congress, and a few negative quotes from gun enthusiasts.

This information served her well when there was an opportunity to use her field reporting to campaign for her cause. She found ample opportunity to use this ammunition as she presented her views on the weekend news.

She wanted to take full advantage of this opportunity to enhance her career and promote her cause. Each carefully crafted statement would be designed to demonstrate that guns are evil and any civil society should prohibit all public firearm ownership.

The next local gun show would be near Warner Robins, Georgia. That was usually considered too far away for a remote broadcast because it is the outer edge of their viewership. Yet, it would not be out of the question. She wanted to go, so she pitched the idea to her boss.

A direct assignment was very unlikely this far in advance, and the best she expected was, "Maybe, if the weekend is completely dead." In spite of the inherent risk, she laid out her proposal.

"Noreen, I have an event that I'd like to cover," she said bluntly.

"Okay, shoot," came the simple reply.

"You remember the 'paintball incident' at a gun show in Norcross a few weeks ago?" she asked rhetorically. "There is another gun show coming up down in Warner Robins. I would like to do a follow-up story on the incident, and another gun show provides an ideal backdrop for both the follow-up story and it fits this new assignment. I would like to weave in some on-site interviews for the new assignment and make the connection back to the paintball stunt. It can be a remote broadcast if it is a slow news weekend or it can be a prerecorded piece.

Noreen looked at her with a penetrating stare and paused. "Sure, why not? That just might work. See what you can come up with," she replied as she started to walk away, signaling the end of their conversation.

Jennifer felt fully empowered and threw herself into the task, even though she was keenly aware that another assignment might come up and prevent her from traveling to Warner Robins. Nonetheless, enthusiasm took control, and she chased after it with genuine excitement.

Chapter 9

In Kansas, the house was dark just as Reggie expected. There was one dim light that he determined must have been on a timer. It had been on and off at the same time each day for a week. Several issues of the local free newspaper lay on the driveway like signal lights announcing that no one was home. The newspapers carried a variety of local business ads, but in the darkness, they advertised that no one had been home for days.

There were other signs as well. No car in the driveway. The lights had not been on in the main part of the house on any of the evenings that week when he had driven by.

Reggie had watched this neighborhood for several weeks. He had looked for the signs of a homeowner away, and this was a classic case. The living room blinds were open day and night. The TV, visible from the street, had not been on any evening.

No signs of any dogs at this house or any of the

adjacent houses. Dogs are a pain, and it wouldn't be good to have a barking dog announcing his presence, even next door.

This was going to be an easy one. He was still very careful. He drove by one more time before he parked over a block away. He would enter and exit in the darkness of the backyard.

He was only looking for cash, jewelry, small electronics or other small items that would fit in his backpack. If he were lucky, he would find cash. He would also be on the lookout for Christmas gifts. He hoped to find electronics that were purchased as gifts, still in the original packing and obviously not registered yet. He would still fence his goods far from the source to add another layer of protection.

This was not Reggie's first robbery, and he had disciplined himself to keep it simple. He would not get greedy. Careful surveillance was the key to his success. He counted on his assumption that detectives in small towns don't have time to run after small breaking and entering cases any more than their counterparts in the city. Take the stuff that's easy and move on to the next gig.

His surveillance was designed to ensure that no one was home, and he would walk away if there were ever any signs of people in the house. He didn't want any confrontations. His only concession was the handgun tucked in his belt near the center of his back. It was only there for an extreme emergency. He would flash it, if needed, and then make his escape.

Reggie didn't want to leave any evidence behind, not even a fingerprint. He had selected shoes that were common and left no detailed print, even in the mud. Every piece of clothing he had on was carefully chosen and was available at dozens of different stores. Nothing unique, he did not want anything to be able to be traced back to him.

The back door was easy to open, even with latex gloves. There were nine small glass panels in the door and an old-fashion deadbolt lock with a thumb handle on the inside. He carefully broke the glass closest to the doorknob and unlocked the deadbolt with a twist. The doorknob was also locked but it unlocked and opened the door with a simple turn. He was always humored at how easy it was to break into older houses. This unit was clearly built in a time when this neighborhood was safe and locks were not really necessary.

He walked quietly through the living room and mentally inventoried the items he would want. The only light needed was provided by the street lamp in front of the house. He noted the latest video game console and knew from experience it would fit in his backpack. The games would not be worth much, but a few games made the list anyway because they made selling the controller easier. He looked at the DVD player and knew it was not worth the effort. TVs were always too big for his plans.

He eased into the short hallway of the small three-bedroom ranch. It was the worst possible scenario. There was someone else in the house, but he didn't know it yet.

David had arrived at the airport early in the evening from an extended business trip. His car had been parked for days and would not start. Then, to make matters worse, it didn't crank when AAA arrived to give him a jumpstart. He decided to have it towed to the local dealer and take care of it some other time. He took a taxi, and it was already late when he finally arrived home. He didn't even unpack at all. He just dumped his luggage on the floor in his bedroom. He was totally exhausted and went straight to bed and crashed.

Reggie was deliberate, but not slow. He thought he was alone in the house when he quietly entered the first room on the left. He was still careful not to make much noise. The bedroom was used as an office of sorts. He checked the desk drawers and the file cabinet. His quick search found only a few dollars in the desk and little else. He stuffed the dollar bills into his jeans' pocket and continued his search. He took extra time with the four-drawer file cabinet, but it didn't yield any valuables.

David was groggy when he rolled over in the bed and opened his eyes. He had not slept very long and his head was foggy. He didn't even know why he was awake. He closed his eyes and waited for sleep to take over again.

Meanwhile, Reggie kept moving and began working his way through the second bedroom. It was used as a storage room and a bedroom. Boxes lined one wall and appeared to have never been unpacked from a move. They were neatly stacked, but didn't give any hint of their contents. He decided not to rummage through them yet. He would return to them if his search didn't produce enough results. So far, this house didn't seem like it was going to yield much.

The closet in the second bedroom had the same metal accordion-style doors as the previous bedroom. However, it made a loud pop sound when he opened it. He cringed and instinctively stopped. His heart was pounding, but that was the only sound he heard.

David's eyes opened wide at the sound. He was momentarily frozen in place, caught somewhere between slumber and consciousness. The fact that he was sound asleep when the door in the next room popped made him wonder if it was just a dream. He listened intently for any other sounds. At first, there was only silence, and he prepared to go back to sleep. He had no idea that someone else was in his house.

The closet door was now open and Reggie peered into the darkness. He carefully pulled his flashlight out of the holster on his belt. It was a small Maglight, just large enough to hold two AA batteries. He twisted it, and the contents of the closet were fully illuminated. He held the light loosely in his mouth, leaving both hands free.

An old metal box the size of a cigar box caught his

eye. He quietly reached for the box and brought it down to eye level. It made a slight noise as the contents shifted, but he was not alarmed. He opened the lid in order to see what treasure he might find inside.

David heard the muffled sounds coming from the spare bedroom. Grogginess obscured his mind. He decided that there might be a rodent loose in the house, so he decided it required some investigation. The possibility of an intruder had not even crossed his mind.

David slid out of bed. Barefoot, he didn't make a sound. He rubbed his eyes and made his way in the dark. He was still only half awake as he made his way toward his bedroom door. At the door, he noticed a faint shadow in the spare bedroom. The presence of an intruder still did not register in his sleepy state. He stepped across the hall and into the doorway of the spare bedroom.

Reggie was completely unaware of David's presence until he looked up from the closet door and saw his silhouette in the doorway. Simultaneously, they both were shocked by the discovery that they were not alone.

The shock flooded David's mind to the point of momentary confusion. In those seconds of pause, Reggie reached for the handgun in his belt. He pulled the gun out and pointed it toward David. His well-thought-out plan to show the gun as a distraction to facilitate his escape went away as he heard the sound of the gun firing and felt the recoil in his hand. The flash from the short barrel seemed even brighter in the darkness. Reggie was shocked. He didn't mean to discharge the weapon. David stumbled backward into his room in part from the impact of the bullet, but mostly from sheer shock.

The sight of blood gushing from David's neck caused Reggie to panic even more. He grabbed the flashlight out of his mouth and shoved it into his pants' pocket. He ran to the back door and fled.

David tried to call out, but was unable to make a sound. He grabbed his throat and headed for the phone. He was surprised by the amount of blood that gushed between his fingers with each heartbeat. He was already lightheaded, and his thoughts were starting to blur. He began to lose consciousness as he reached the foot of the bed. He didn't even feel the fall. Death followed shortly after he hit the floor.

Reggie was still in shock when he reached his car. The petty thief became a murderer that night; he just didn't know it yet.

He tossed the gun's cylinder assembly, complete with the unfired bullets, from a bridge into a deep part of a river as he made his way home. The remaining gun frame was tossed into a solitary lake along his route.

His mind raced as he replayed all of his steps. Were his precautions enough? Surely the investigation of a shooting would be different than a break-in. Had he made enough mistakes to get caught? Would running far away help?

He decided to never return to the scene, not even the town. The sound of a man staggering backward haunted him as he drove. The bright mussel flash blinded him in the darkness, and he did not see the impact of the bullet. He wondered if the scene would always be so vivid in his mind.

Chapter 10

The phone rang twice before a steady voice answered, "9-1-1, what's your emergency?"

Two patrol units from the small police department were dispatched to the address. They were given the necessary information and the words "possible shots fired" were repeated twice in the radio communication to ensure that the officers knew what they might encounter. The officers proceeded with caution.

When they reached the master bedroom they found the victim, motionless on the floor in a pool of blood. They radioed what they found. The dead body was not disturbed except to check for any sign of life. There was none.

The next few hours were dedicated to collecting and processing anything that might be evidence. This was now a homicide investigation. A senior detective was assigned to the case and took control as soon as he arrived. The coroner was dispatched to the scene.

Hours later the work was still underway. The body was identified as the occupant of the house and the next-of-kin were identified as the parents of the 32 year-old victim. Their residence was in another jurisdiction, and officers from that area would make the death notification.

The body was photographed from every angle before it was moved. As with any homicide, an autopsy would be required. The body was taken to the local morgue.

Joseph Brandenburg, the lead detective, instinctively processed all the evidence as it was being gathered. Experience had been an excellent teacher, and he had been a good student. His initial assessment was that this was a break-in gone wrong. He did not mention his assessment to anyone. He simply pondered the fact, analyzed the evidence, processed the crime scene as a whole, and everything pointed to a lone intruder, surprised by the deceased.

What wasn't clear was the reason for the violence. The evidence didn't indicate a struggle, but the victim was shot at close range. Things were not ransacked. Nothing big was missing.

There was work to be done, but he guessed the perpetrator left no fingerprints. He also did not expect much other forensic evidence. The crime scene was not likely to offer much help. He would follow every lead and every tip, but he had seen his share of crime scenes, and this one was not filled with evidence that would point them to specific suspects.

Later that same morning, in a town not far away, two uniformed officers knocked on the Henderson's front door. They confirmed that they were speaking to Mr. Henderson, the father of David Michael Henderson. Then the officer made a simple and direct statement, "Mr. Henderson, I am sorry to inform you that David has died. He was shot and killed in his home." The officer paused for a moment. He had delivered this type of news before and knew to expect just about anything.

Mr. Henderson was quiet. The words were still sinking in. Then he calmly asked, "Are you sure?"

The officer responded, "Yes sir." After a brief pause he added, "You or some other next-of-kin will need to confirm the identity in person."

Mr. Henderson nodded his consent. He was visibly shaken, but remained stoic. The next several hours were a blur for Mr. and Mrs. Henderson.

It was mid-morning by the time they returned home. They began the difficult task of telling others what had happened. The first calls would be to David's sisters.

It was Saturday morning about 11:30 a.m. when Helen answered the phone. Her father broke the terrible news to her. Tears filled her eyes as she listened. She could barely speak. The conversation was not long, and when it was over, she simply sat down and wept.

Helen cried for a long time. Memories flooded her mind with images of David. She immediately thought of their last time together. It had been only a few weeks. David had scheduled an extended layover in Atlanta just to have time with her. They had met for dinner. She had no idea that it would be the last time she would see him alive.

She replayed the event in her mind and wondered if she had said the right things. Did she tell him how much she loved him?

They were close as children. She had many memories of their antics growing up together on the farm. The years had taken their lives in different directions, and yet their closeness endured despite the distance and decreased time together.

Her heart was heavy. She struggled to comprehend the horrible news. There were many unanswered questions, but Why? seemed to scream the loudest. Why David? Why not someone else?

Chapter 11

Helen needed someone close by to turn to, to lean on. She thought of Kent, but wanted and needed to know more about him. She liked him; she just didn't know much about him.

She thought of calling him to tell him about David's death. She wondered if she should and wondered if he would want to know. He didn't know David, and he never would. She didn't want to burden him with something so personal, but she wanted someone close by to be there for her. An internal conflict continued to nag at her.

She sought to escape the pain by surfing the Internet. She searched several places and then landed on Bree Security Consulting's site. It was a simple, well laid out website. She navigated around examining each section with curiosity and increasing personal interest.

"The Team" link showed a picture of each consultant along with his or her credentials and experience. Kent's picture topped the list. It was a recent photo and made a favorable impression. Under his image it stated:

> Kent Bree, founder and CEO of Bree Security Consulting (BSC), leads a team of experienced security consultants.

The other consultants were listed along with their specialty. It was an impressive group. Their photos were professionally presented. Their experience was varied, as were their credentials. The site was clearly designed to impress potential clients.

The "About Us" page stated:

A team approach is the cornerstone of the BSC philosophy. Our strength is in the strategically aligned expertise of our team. Clients work with one consultant, but all team members are involved with the evaluation of each client's needs. This joint effort ensures that everyone at BSC is directly invested in our service to each client. This level of commitment is unmatched in the security industry.

Helen was impressed with the company and its website. Nonetheless, her questions remained unanswered. Should she call him or not? If so, what would she say?

She debated with herself for quite some time. Her indecision threatened to lead her to do nothing. Then, almost on a whim, she grabbed her phone and dialed his number.

She didn't plan what to say; she just called. He

answered quickly and caught her somewhat off guard.

"Hello Helen. I was thinking about you."

She momentarily forgot that his cell phone would automatically identify her number and she thought, How did he know it was me? She responded quietly, "Hey there Kent. I've been thinking about you, too."

He heard something different in her voice and inquired, "Is something wrong?"

"Yes," she said, fighting to maintain her composure. She held her breath for just a moment. Then she heard herself say, "My brother was killed! Somebody broke in and shot him dead."

Kent was shocked, but his response was rock solid. "Helen," he offered tenderly, "is there anyone there with you?"

"No." A quiver in her voice was evident even in her one word answer.

"I'm glad you called me. Would it be okay if I came over for a while? I don't want you to be alone."

"Would you? I feel like I'm imposing on you."

He didn't hesitate and immediately volunteered, "I'll be right over. You certainly don't need to feel bad about calling me." Kent had already begun to quietly prepare to leave. "I am honored that you would call me at such an important time."

"My father called a little while ago with the news. I'm so sorry to burden you, but I just need someone to talk to."

"I'm on my way." He continued to speak tenderly to her, with genuine compassion. He, too, knew the pain of losing someone close. Though he had only seen her at the party and then at dinner, he had hoped their relationship would grow. He felt like he had known her for years. He had already told her things about himself that he seldom revealed to anyone. Their friendship was special, and he knew it.

He drove faster than usual in an effort to get to her as quickly as possible. When he arrived at her condo, he parked his car out front and hurried to the door.

Helen opened the door. Swollen, red eyes gave evidence of the tears that had already been shed. Kent opened his arms and she leaned into him. He held her close as she quietly cried.

Their embrace was long and gave Helen time to collect herself. Her emotions were still raw, and she would struggle from time to time as the afternoon turned into evening. In the future, she would look back at the significance of their time together that day and recognize how much their relationship grew during those tender hours. His gentleness and compassion was much more than she had anticipated. He gently held her hand at times as they talked. She felt safe and openly confided in him.

The conversation aimlessly meandered from topic to topic as the hours passed. They both talked about childhood experiences and what life was like "back then."

Helen would occasionally turn the conversation back to David as she relived significant shared experiences. Some brought tears to her eyes and others made her laugh out loud. Talking about David was like a healing medicine.

Kent spoke of life growing up in a small town. He confessed that some of the restraint from doing wrong during his early teen years came from a fear of being seen by someone in town. Word was sure to get back to his parents and he knew what his dad would do. Fear, he noted with a smile, was an effective motivator.

He told funny stories on himself and his friends. He told her about a close friend named Ray. They did almost everything together until they both went to college. Ray was like a brother, and their friendship endured even after years of living separate lives.

Dinner was delivered by the local Chinese restaurant. Their conversation was deep at times, and yet, never uncomfortable. Kent listened well and Helen needed someone to talk with.

As the evening became night, Helen wondered how it would end. She dreaded being alone again, but knew Kent was not the type to stay the night with her. He was a complete gentleman, and she knew he would hold her to comfort her in her grief, but would not take it any further.

They talked into the early morning hours. As time passed, words were replaced with silence. They both knew it was time for him to go, but neither wanted to break it off.

Finally, Kent quietly said, "You need some rest."

She knew he was right and responded, "Yes I know I do. Thank you so much. You have been a good friend to me today."

They walked to the door in silence. Kent slipped on his coat and opened the door. As he started to leave he said, "I'll call you in the morning."

She watched as he walked away toward his car. Her heart still ached, but the pain was different now. She knew for sure that there was more to learn about this man, but today, he had touched her heart. He helped her begin the difficult process of healing.

Chapter 12

Reggie played the sequence of events over and over in his mind. He had learned of the man's fate on the TV news. "Dead from a single gunshot wound to the neck," were the reporter's words. Reggie was shocked when he heard them. He did not know his victim and didn't want to know him. A man was dead, and he was the killer.

He thought of numerous mistakes he had made that night and expected the police to arrive any day. He dwelt on his actions, reviewing them one by one.

He wondered if he had been seen. As he mulled it over in his mind, it was not so much, if he had been seen, but how many people must have seen him? Perhaps a curious neighbor or someone he had not observed had seen him. Maybe someone noticed his car. Surely the police would hear from someone who saw him.

He performed a careful analysis of every step. His reconnaissance had been thorough. What had he missed? No one seemed to be at home. There were no signs that anyone had been there in days, none. The house had every sign of an empty house. So where did this guy come from?

He had always taken extra precautions. Gloves prevented fingerprints. Common clothing and shoes made sure that they could not be easily tracked back to him. Everything he had seen or heard that could give away his identity was carefully and thoughtfully disguised. Where had things gone so dreadfully wrong?

The stress of constant vigilance ate away at his nerves. He lived in fear that he would somehow reveal his dark secret to someone, even by accident. It took a toll on him both physically and, even more so, mentally.

Nights were long and sleep evaded him. Shadows closed in and seemed to suck all the air out of any room. The bright mussel flash of his gun firing in the dark still blinded him, just as it had the night the guy died. Fear of being caught choked him like an overpowering force wrapped around his neck in the darkness.

At times, the pressure was so heavy he thought of turning himself in and ending this thing once and for all. Guilt mixed with regret weighed him down. He wished he could do it all over again and not fire his weapon this time. If he had just run, things would be different. Why did he pull out the gun? How had it fired?

He wanted to escape and spent long hours playing mind-numbing video games. Every night was long. He wanted to escape the torture of endless hours of questioning and review.

Life was not the same, and he somehow knew it never would be. Taking someone's life was not in his plans. He could justify stealing and could even live with himself as a thief. Killing someone was not the same. He had crossed a line and now some poor soul was dead. As much as he wanted to, there was no way to go back.

The fact remained, the man was dead, and he was now more than a thief.

Chapter 13

Helen's cell phone rang and she looked to see who it was before she answered. It was Kent, and she quickly touched the screen to take his call.

"Well, hello there," she smiled as she spoke.

"Hello. How are you doing today?"

"I'm doing better, glad you called. I was afraid that I might have unloaded too much on you yesterday."

"I was glad you called and let me know," he confided. "It meant a lot to me that you would allow me such a privilege."

"You made a tough day much better. Thank you."

"You are very welcome. Do you want to get out for the afternoon? Perhaps we could go somewhere for a late lunch?" his optimistic tone was obvious.

"Sure, what do you have in mind?" she asked. "It would be good to get out for a while."

"There is a small diner not too far from where you are that has a quiet atmosphere. It is not a fancy dining experience, but the food is excellent. Does that sound good to you?"

"Sure," she remarked with a hint of sadness in her voice. "Count me in." Then she asked, "How much time do I have to get ready?"

"How much time do you need?" he teased.

She responded quickly, "Give me an hour and I'll be ready to go."

"Okay then, I'll be there in 60 minutes," he continued to tease.

"Oh ... I'd better hurry. See ya soon. Goodbye."

Before he could respond, she hung up. Kent looked at his phone and decided she was serious. He grinned at the thought of her hurrying around to get ready. He thought, I hope she knows that this is truly casual dining.

Exactly 60 minutes later, Kent knocked on her door. He didn't mean to rush her, and he felt a little mischievous arriving so promptly. He didn't really expect her to be ready, but she answered the door and immediately announced, "I'm starving."

"Well, let's go then," he replied without missing a beat.

She was dressed in jeans with a light blue blouse that matched her shoes and jacket. She had listened for details as Kent described the restaurant, but he hadn't give much information. She decided that jeans were "casual" and she didn't feel like dressing up anyway.

Kent was impressed. Her casual look was more than he expected. To him, she looked great; he noticed the woman more than the matching outfit.

The Sunday afternoon drive to the restaurant was filled with signs of the approaching Christmas season. The decoration helped lighten the otherwise heavy mood. They chatted along the way and both recognized a growing comfort level that comes with a maturing friendship.

They were seated immediately. The booth gave the feeling of privacy, and they talked about work and things they did for fun. It was not obvious, but they avoided the topic of family. David was not mentioned. Kent enjoyed giving his suggestions as they talked about the menu options.

"You've been here more than once," she noted.

"Oh yes, I know good food when I taste it," he responded with a grin.

Playfully, she inquired, "Well, mister experience, what do you recommend?"

"You can't go wrong with anything. It is all very tasty." He sounded like a sales rep. "My favorite is the breakfast offerings. The daily special is also a good choice. If you like pie, save room for the peach cobbler."

"Okay, you sold me on the breakfast. If it is half as good as you say, I'd be foolish to try anything else."

"You won't be disappointed. I promise."

The food did not disappoint. Helen enjoyed every bite, but could not finish her plate.

The conversation stayed light while they ate. Helen wondered if she was flirting like a schoolgirl, but she really didn't care. She was having a good time, distracted from the focus on death, and it showed.

Kent was glad to provide a welcome distraction from the pain and sorrow that was never far away. The meal was an excuse to spend time with Helen. He knew that she knew. The feeling was mutual.

The mood slowly became more somber as they drove back toward Helen's place. The reprieve had been helpful, but all too brief.

"When do you leave to go back home?" he inquired gently as they neared her neighborhood.

"I fly out next Saturday morning, December 22." She didn't offer any more information. Kent offered to take her to the airport and she gladly accepted. Her thoughts, however, were somewhere else as she stared at the scenery passing by outside.

When they arrived, she looked at Kent. The weight of her loss was now visible on her face again. He wanted to wipe it all away, but death cannot be brushed aside that easily.

They sat quietly in the car for a while. He gently held her hand in his. The moment did not merit words, not because any comment would be inadequate, but because the tenderness spoke volumes. He was there for her, walking down the otherwise lonesome road of grief. His companionship was more than she expected, and his sensitivity helped lessen her deep pain with his tender care.

The day had been much more than a meal shared by friends. It was more than a date in a budding relationship. It put their relationship on the fast track. Trust grew. Intimacy was experienced by both, even though holding hands and enjoying a long embrace was as far as their physical relationship had gone.

Death had intruded in the early days of their relationship. It could have been a wedge; instead, it plowed the ground for the seed of deep, abiding love. Tears had watered it, and it was beginning to bud.

Chapter 14

The information Helen received from her father's call about David's death was very limited. In his mind, he was doing his best to protect her. His motives were pure, but Helen wanted answers.

As the days passed, she yearned for the truth. The Why? hung around, demanding an answer. It just wouldn't go away.

She was actually glad when the detective leading the investigation called. He was merely following every possible lead and called her as he did everyone connected to the victim.

He began by identifying himself, "My name is Joseph Brandenburg. I am a detective with the police department investigating the death of David Michael Henderson. Could I ask you a few questions?"

Helen swallowed hard before she could respond. She simply said, "Yes, of course."

"Are you Helen Henderson, David's sister?"

"Yes, I am his older sister."

"I know this is difficult, but any information you can give us will help with the investigation."

"I want to help in any way I can," she said with genuine sincerity.

"Thank you," he said without much emotion. He moved quickly on with his work. "Well, I won't take a lot of your time. When was the last time you saw David?"

"It was just a few weeks ago. We had dinner together here in Atlanta." This was more difficult than she thought, but she continued, "David planned a long layover on one of his business trips, and I picked him up at the airport. We had a nice meal together at 'The Pecan.' It's a restaurant near the airport. I took him back to the airport to catch his next flight."

"Did you talk to David on a regular basis?"

"No, we talked from time to time, but I wouldn't say it was regular," she responded, barely holding her emotions in check.

Brandenburg read her emotions, even over the phone. He took some time to talk about something else before he continued with questions. "Our records indicate that David was originally from Kansas. I suppose that is farm country, right?" he offered to ease the tension.

"Yes sir," she replied. She instinctively reverted to

the polite, respectful rhetoric of her younger days.

He prefaced his next questions with another routine line about how difficult this must be. He sounded genuine, though he had used the same line many times before. "Do you know anyone who might have a reason to harm your brother?" Before she could answer, he continued, "Do you know anyone, perhaps a friend, someone he worked with, or even a family member, that may have been upset with David over something he might have done?"

Helen waited for a short time before she answered. She didn't need the extra time to think, but rather wanted time to ensure she was composed. "No. I don't know anyone who had a problem with anything he did. David was kind and gentle. He was easygoing. He traveled a lot in his work, so I wouldn't know anything about the people he worked with."

She became a bit defensive when she talked about family. "We have a close, loving family. There isn't any relative who didn't love David."

The detective sensed the genuineness in her response. Yet, he knew he needed to ask more questions. As the dialog progressed, Helen realized that this might be her only opportunity to learn more about what really happened that night.

She bluntly, but meekly asked, "May I ask you a few questions?"

"Why certainly." He knew he would learn more about what she might know or suspect from her questions, probably more than he would learn from the questions he might pose, so he welcomed her inquiry.

She started with a very general question, "What happened that night? No one has told me anything."

Brandenburg wasn't surprised by the question. He had heard this one, or other versions of it, many times. He began with the standard speech about "an ongoing investigation," and he truthfully added that they had "very little to go on." He preferred to have this type of conversation in person so he could read facial expressions and body language. He was clearly at a disadvantage, but he could never justify the cost of traveling to Atlanta just to interview a relative. He made a split-second decision to take a risk and reveal some of the facts in the case. He knew he didn't have much to go on now, so he concluded it wouldn't hurt.

"Your brother was shot by a 38-caliber bullet," he paused to take a breath, "apparently at close range. The bullet severed the carotid artery on the left side of his neck, and we believe he died very quickly. The coroner placed the time of death between 2 and 3 a.m. There is no evidence that any other shots were fired."

He paused again, giving her a chance to respond and providing him the opportunity to listen for any sounds she might make. Hearing nothing, he moved on, "There was no evidence of a struggle. He was found in the master bedroom, and there were no lights on anywhere in the house when the police arrived."

Helen was emboldened by the apparent progress she was making. She asked, "What else can you tell me about what happened?"

"We are following up on every lead, but we do not have a suspect at this time."

"So you don't know who did this?" she stated more than asked. There was no hint of anger or frustration in her voice.

"Not at this time," he candidly replied. "One theory we have is that your brother surprised a thief who was already in the house and was shot by the intruder."

"Is there anything I can do to help?" she inquired.

His fishing expedition didn't produce any results. This seems like a dead end. He thought to himself.

"If you think of anyone who might have wanted to harm your brother for any reason, please let me know immediately." He gave her his contact information and encouraged her to call with anything she might recall in the future. He thanked her for her assistance and ended the call.

Brandenburg made a few notes for the file, but knew this was just a routine call he had to make to complete the file. He still believed his original theory, and the investigation was not turning up any new evidence or any credible leads. He feared this investigation was headed for the "unsolved" file drawer. Time was not on his side. He knew that if something didn't turn up soon, this case would suffer the fate of so many that had no clear direction. The continuous flood of cases left little time to invest in a case that had stalled.

Helen was still in shock. The detective's description left her with more questions than answers. She yearned for more facts. Most of all, she wanted to know who shot and killed her brother.

She began to search for more information and investigated every detail that she could find. It took a while, but her mind wanted answers as much as her heart. The quest for information drove her to search every possible source, but the distance from the scene left her with little more than search engines on the Internet. News articles were too superficial to satisfy, yet there seemed to be little else.

Then she stumbled on one of the many gun control bloggers that mentioned her brother. She discovered the comments that followed. Like many blogs, the comments and associated links were interconnected in a seemingly random fashion. They supplied an almost never-ending chain of commentary.

She had little previous exposure to the gun control

debate. The rhetoric of the gun control advocates and their condemnation of the senseless violence caused by guns caught her attention, and she read every word with deep emotional interest.

As she read, she began to agree with them and their disdain for guns. She embraced their reproach of the proliferation of guns and the harm guns inflicted on innocent victims. It seemed to make sense. Guns kill. There was no way for her to escape that fact. Her brother was dead. He was the victim of a violent death caused by a gun. She wanted to direct her rage at something. The fact that she did not have a suspect to be the target of her rage generated a subtle, hidden frustration. She jumped at the chance to place the blame somewhere. Guns were the first easy target to blame, especially the gun that killed David, her brother.

She read on, devouring the text as if she were driven by starvation. Fury about his murder, mixed with defense for him as an innocent person, invoked powerful emotions. She read more and more of the gun control blogs and the comment chains that followed.

As she waded deeper into the content, her emotions began to change. She realized that the more she read, the more she began to turn against the gun control advocates.

It started as she remembered growing up on a farm where guns were as common as farm tools. She remembered that her own father had taught her to use and respect firearms. He was a gentle man, and yet he knew the value of guns. Helen and her siblings learned these lessons well. They all knew how to handle a handgun, rifle or shotgun.

David knew how to handle a firearm. His death at the hands of a gun was not the gun's fault; it was the gun in the hands of a killer.

The ire within her began to build as she continued to read. Her brother's death was nothing more than fodder for their rants. They didn't know him, yet they spoke of him and other victims as casualties in their war. Each new death by gunfire became an excuse to lash out. Victims were nothing more than ammunition used against their enemies.

Her pain slowly turned to resolve. She would not dishonor David's death by playing their blame game. She hated the way they exploited his death. David was not the person they described. He would not want his name used to promote their agenda against guns. He was not a victim of guns; he was murdered in cold blood by a person who used a gun. To Helen, the distinction was critical.

The resolve took root. She decided that day to arm herself, to purchase a gun for personal protection and to learn to handle it well. She would not be a defenseless victim.

Helen turned her thoughts to David, the person she missed. She wanted to celebrate his life. It was the antidote for mourning. She remembered so many good times and she wanted to cherish those memories.

One significant step in that direction was the development of a website that would serve to eulogize and honor David's life. There were several sites she considered, and she selected an easy, preformatted one. Her focus was on David and his legacy, not a complex presentation.

The aspect that pleased her most was the electronic guestbook. Over the coming days, there would be entries from family, extended family and close friends. Their comments were medicine for the injured heart. What surprised her most was the wide range of people who visited the site and took time to write. Some were those they had not heard from in years. Others she didn't even know, but were individuals who had some connection to David, his old friends and new.

Her father had been told that an autopsy would need to be performed and that his body would be released to the mortuary as soon as it was completed. He was told to plan on 48 to 72 hours. With that in mind, a memorial service for David was planned by his parents for the days between Christmas and New Year's.

This would be a formal goodbye and provide some needed closure. Helen already planned to be in Kansas at her sister's for the holidays. This was not what she planned for, but it was how they would spend those days.

Some questions would always remain unanswered, but they all knew they needed to close this chapter of their lives. David would have insisted that they move on. Life was too precious to linger too long over his death.

Still, the unanswered question of Who did this? would not go away. A life had ended suddenly and prematurely. It demanded an answer and yet, there was none.

Chapter 15

Ray was not surprised when Kent called. Their friendship began in elementary school and was founded upon the shared experiences of growing up together. It had been years since they had seen each other, but he was still glad to spend time with an old friend.

The depth of their relationship was forged during their high school days. Those truly were the good old days. They shared the full array of experiences from classes and football, to girls and life dreams.

After high school, their careers took them in vastly different directions, yet their friendship had endured. It had been nurtured along by brief conversations on the rare occasions when their paths crossed. Yet, somehow, it was as deep today as it was more than twenty-five years ago when they lined up together on a small town high school football team.

Kent's army career was mostly in Special Forces, and his assignments had taken him to many unnamed places where he was asked to do things he couldn't talk about. Ray enjoyed spending time with him partly because Kent's life was everything that his was not—a life of travel to exotic places filled with danger and intrigue. The years were filled with experiences that others only read about.

Kent's current career was a direct result of his army days. He owned his own consulting firm, specializing in security. The majority of his initial work focused on security for special events, but the business has grown to derive its income from consultations with a variety of businesses that wanted an independent evaluation of their security. This was the future for Kent's business, and he embraced it and had added staff accordingly.

His business had been very successful. The protection business had grown in the aftermath of 9/11. It had not been difficult to expand into new areas. Many of his existing clients had requested help in additional areas, and Kent simply responded to needs, usually by adding new staff. He had hired most of his team from his former colleagues from Special Forces.

The most recent new work came as one of his top clients was sending a wave of high-level personnel to other countries to live and work. The company had sought help from Kent and his team. This was one of Kent's areas of expertise. His experience had prepared him well to advise those preparing for life abroad.

Kent had called Ray and said he was going to be up near where Ray worked and suggested that they meet for coffee. Ray said he would be able to leave work early the next afternoon, and they agreed to meet not far from Ray's office in Marietta.

The coffee shop was actually quite large. It was laid out somewhat like a maze and provided a variety of semiprivate nooks for quiet conversation. Kent got there early and already had a coffee cup in his hand when Ray arrived.

"Ray, good to see you."

"You too, Kent, it's been a while."

"What would you like to drink?" Kent asked. "They have coffee just about any way you want it."

"I'll have a large cup of black coffee. That's all."

Kent seemed amused by Ray's choice as he replied, "I guess I should have known."

Ray had always been the one who lived in the same small town they had grown up in. Kent loved to rag on Ray about living a boring life, but he really respected Ray for his commitment to conservative values, especially his family. Army life had been hard on marriages, and Kent didn't have many friends that had been able to make it work. He saw Ray as the classic country boy who never really left the country, except to go to college and then to work. He still lived on a hundred acres, commuted to a job in the city, and was back home every evening to tend to his chores.

Kent handed Ray a large black coffee and said, "Here's your boring brew."

"How are things in your world?" Ray asked with genuine interest.

"Well, work's been good," he answered in a way that said I don't really want to talk about anything personal. "I've had more than enough work to stay busy. But, with the holidays coming, it will slack off until after New Year's."

"You still like it?"

"Oh, yeah. There is enough variety to keep me interested."

"Do you still travel a lot?" To Ray it seemed that Kent always arranged to spend most of his life on the road somewhere, and he was a little surprised by Kent's reply.

"I don't travel as much as I used to. It gets old, you know."

Ray responded with the first thing that came to mind, "I'm sure it does." Of course, Kent knew that Ray had no idea what it was like to live out of a suitcase and wake up in a hotel room each morning.

"What about you?" Kent redirected. "I guess you're still living out in Ellijay on your low maintenance farm."

"Yeah, I'm enjoying the good life. I've got my farming chores down to a minimum." Ray responded with complete candor. He was torn between the extra work required to raise cattle. Although cattle can provide extra income, it was never about the money for Ray. "I love the extra space, especially during deer season. I guess I like having my own land to hunt on."

"So how many head of cattle do you have now?

"I've only got twenty-two now. I averaged almost 250 a year a few years back, but it's just too much work. I've found better ways to spend my time. I keep thinking about loading them all up and taking them to the market. It just isn't worth the effort for so few."

Kent quizzed Ray about his family and they talked about what each of Ray's daughters was doing. He commented how they seemed to have grown up so quickly. Ray admitted that he felt the same way.

Ray wondered about Kent's situation, but decided not to ask. He knew that Kent's first marriage didn't last and neither did his second. As far as he knew, Kent never had any kids and the thought made him feel sorry for him. He wondered if Kent was lonely, but kept his thoughts to himself.

In spite of the fact that they were so different, there was still a depth to their friendship that neither would ever be able to explain. They had known each other a long time, and neither felt it necessary to be anything but himself when they were together. That provided a firm foundation for their relationship. The glue, however, was made of mutual respect.

Ray knew Kent as a real man, a soldier. Not only had he always kept himself in excellent physical condition, but he never tried to make it an issue. In the early years, he may have stayed in shape because it was a requirement of his assigned duty; however, he was still just as fit now.

Kent saw Ray as one of the few people he could really trust. This placed Ray in a small group of people that Kent usually reserved for those he had faced danger with. Kent saw Ray as the quintessential American, honest, hardworking and loyal. He was the kind of man Kent was proud to have as a friend.

The conversation migrated from topic to topic and back again. Ray asked as many questions about Kent's work, past and present, as he thought he could get away with. Kent's life was certainly more interesting than most.

Kent talked about his security consulting business for a while. He explained that in most cases it was not necessary for a business to guard against every possible threat. It was important to identify the areas of greatest risk.

"However," he said, like a teacher speaking to his student, "the greatest cost is often not in the dollars spent but in other losses. For example, how do you quantify the cost when employees no longer feel safe at work? How much will it cost to rebuild consumer confidence if you ever lose it?"

Ray was surprised to hear Kent say, "The underlying principle we market for site security is that you want to make things secure enough that the threat will choose an easier target. Then the focus can be placed on the internal sense of security."

"That sounds simple enough," Ray observed. He was not just being a good student; he was actually enjoying the lesson.

Kent nodded as if to say, it really is that simple. He then posed a question that caught Ray a bit off guard, "What do you think our most difficult clients tend to do?"

Ray pondered the question for a while. Then Kent gave him the answer. "It is the client who cannot identify any potential threats. The easy ones are those who see the threats. We want to focus on being proactive and not reactive. So, identifying the potential risk is essential."

"So you market your work toward those who know what they want to guard against?"

"Yes, because if they already see threats, they will most likely see the others that we will identify in our research that they have missed."

"What do you do with those who don't see any?"

"Well, honestly, we try to avoid them. But, when

we are faced with a client who does not perceive any threats, we conduct a risk assessment, like we would with any client. Our report, like always, is then tailored to their situation."

"But I can think of a lot of potential clients who are clueless that they even have any security risks," Ray commented, as if he were thinking out loud.

"Would you mind naming a few? I'd be interested in what you come up with."

Ray responded immediately, without having to think. "There are any number of large gatherings of people that don't have their eye on security. For example, there are the really big churches. I doubt that most of them have given much thought to security beyond locking the door when no one is there. Another example is the old-fashioned county fairs. They still happen in some county seat town almost every week, but they appear to only focus on shoplifting and other theft-related security issues. I doubt they have ever thought about terrorism or other larger threats."

Kent was impressed with Ray's insights. "Our firm has never been contacted by any size church. You are probably right, it just isn't on their radar."

The conversation continued for a while, but Kent changed his focus from a conversation with an old friend, and began to think about Ray as a potential consultant on his team. He did not mention anything to Ray, but he already instinctively knew he would be a good fit. Most of all, Kent looked for

Unforeseen Impact

team members he could trust and Ray had earned that years ago.

Chapter 16

The conversation with Kent was nothing special. That was Ray's opinion. Later that evening, Ray's wife, Barbara, asked what it was about.

"Oh, nothing special," Ray answered honestly. "We did the usual catching up and talked about old times."

"Well, how's he doing?"

"He's the same as always, I guess."

"Is he married again?" she asked with an inquisitive look.

"No, at least he didn't say he was. I never asked him directly, but if he were, he's not likely to leave out that detail."

"He sure has been a good friend, even after all these years," she commented.

"Yep," Ray agreed, and simultaneously signaled that he was finished talking about his meeting with

Kent. Barbara knew he wanted to do a few chores around the barn, and she was not offended.

Ray went about his evening routine. It was already dark outside, but he was used to getting around after the sun was down. He had installed two mercury-vapor lights that gave plenty of light around the barn. He had carefully calculated the cost of purchase, installation, and the ongoing cost of operation. It was the logical thing to do.

He checked on his livestock and made sure things were ready for the night. It was more like therapy than work. Ray enjoyed the routine, the animals and the general upkeep. His chores changed with the seasons, and he had gradually reduced things in recent years. Now he just did it for exercise and to avoid watching too much TV.

He heard an unusual noise coming from the field behind the barn. He froze in place and listened. It sounded like something had stirred up the cows. Maybe that pesky coyote again, he thought.

He returned to the house and retrieved his high-powered flashlight and his .22 rifle. He slung the rifle over his shoulder and tested the light.

Barbara heard him in the house and inquired, "What ya doin?"

"Sounds like that old coyote is back. I won't be long."

"Okay, just be careful," she said in a motherly tone.

He left the house without saying another word.

Ray grew up around guns. They were as common in his world as a knife, fork and spoon are in a kitchen. He could never imagine a world without them.

His family introduced him to firearms. His mother and father both handled them with confidence. They used them as they would any tool in the house. Ray had seen his mother use a gun almost as frequently as he had seen his father and uncles use one. In fact, his mother was as good a shot with a pistol as any man he knew, a fact he never bothered to point out to his father.

Guns had many uses. Hunting topped the list for most of his friends. However, like many people he knew personally, Ray had at least one firearm close at hand just about everywhere he went. A Glock 19 .40 caliber hung on the bedpost nearest his head every night. He felt it was his duty to protect his family from any intruder.

Ray did not think of himself as an advocate of gun rights and the Second Amendment. However, he did remembered counting more than just a handful of his friends and relatives who went out and got their license to carry a concealed weapon in the first six weeks after Obama was elected president and before he was inaugurated. Handguns, rifles and shotguns were traded among friends and were a common topic at any gathering.

The .22 rifle was for general use around the farm. It

was powerful enough to kill small animals that became a nuisance. It was also lightweight and easy to carry. Most of all, it was accurate. A long barrel was part of the equation, but a small scope made it easy to hit a small target from a fair distance.

He walked quietly toward the barn, listening carefully as he crossed the yard. All was quiet now, but he was going to check it out anyway. The fencepost closest to the barn made a perfect place to scan the field and provided a steady support for taking aim.

He turned on the light with it already pointed in the general direction of the sound. A pair of eyes glowed in the distance. He drew the rifle into position and used the scope to take a closer look. The animal was small, despite the magnification of the scope.

Ray was confident in his accuracy at that distance. The only problem was that the bullet might carry too far if he did miss, and he was mindful of what else might be downrange. He would not take the risk. He watched carefully, but ultimately decided that the coyote was of no real danger to his livestock.

He lowered the gun and turned off the light. Had it been daylight, the outcome might have been different. He retreated to the house and returned the gun and light to their place.

Chapter 17

Atlanta's Hartsfield-Jackson Airport is the world's busiest airport. It averages about ninety million passengers each year, and to Clarke, it seemed that most of them traveled on Christmas Eve.

Crowds always bothered Clarke. Therefore, he didn't enjoy anything about traveling, especially during the peak of the holiday rush. Online purchases relieved him of the need to negotiate the hordes at the mall, but he couldn't avoid the travel. He had even considered driving to Connecticut just to avoid the people.

He checked his bag and begrudgingly paid the extra fee. He made a mental note to never check a bag again. Money was really not the issue; it was waiting in another line that annoyed him.

The initial line for security was long, but moved steadily. The cue reminded him of cattle plodding along in their final march. The movement of two lines side-by-side made the experience seem to pass more quickly.

At the end of the queue they were shuffled into short lines for one of the TSA agents. He showed the agent his boarding pass and driver's license. The agent looked at them and then took a long look at Clarke. It was long enough to make Clarke wonder what he might be thinking. Then he quickly made his marks and Clarke was on his way to the next step in the security process.

Clarke wondered about what would be considered a terrorist threat by these agents. He couldn't help noticing the mindless compliance he observed in the other passengers. Each one began removing their coat and shoes, placing their belongings in bins, and waiting their turn to pass through the metal detector while TSA agents stared straight at them. This last part of the security process made Clarke nervous. He wasn't sure why, he was just glad when it was all over. He collected his things and moved on.

He rode the long escalator down to the train. When the doors opened, he boarded the train along with the rest of the crowd. The second stop was his destination. He exited quickly as if he would somehow escape the crowd and proceeded to the long escalator ride up to the concourse. It quickly filled with others making their way to their gates.

The "B" concourse was busy with holiday travelers. There were quite a few families with kids, more than any other travel season. Clarke looked for a solitary place to wait for his flight; of course, it was a pointless search. He silently withdrew into his private world created by the ear buds inserted in each ear. His eyes focused on the mindless repetition of the game he played of his smart phone as the music drowned out the world around him.

Time passed slowly. He spoke to no one and was glad when they finally began to board his flight.

The flight from Atlanta had been uneventful. He didn't talk to anyone accept to ask the flight attendant for a ginger ale and peanuts. A window seat, always his first choice, allowed for a self-imposed isolation. He remained in his seat for the duration.

He arrived at his parent's house after about a half-hour drive from the airport. The backseat was comfortable, and he tried to have a polite conversation with his parents, whom had both made the trip to the airport to pick him up. It was late afternoon when they arrived at his parent's home.

West Hartford, Connecticut, was not Clarke's home; he had never lived there. It was just the place where his parents lived now. They were proud of where they had decided to retire and were glad to point out the benefits of living there: two hours from New York City and all the city has to offer, a community where the median family income was above $100,000, a town that was number fifty-five on Money Magazine's best places to live, and a progressive state that matched their liberal philosophy. Clarke was not impressed.

In the Nelson household, Christmas vacation was a

time to be endured, not enjoyed. Clarke still didn't know why he accepted the invitation. He would tell himself it was for his mother, but that was only partially true, at best. This was not something to be looked forward to, not with either of his parents. He would tolerate the days and then gladly return to his solitary lifestyle.

Clarke's parents were definitely not poor, and their house was a bold statement about their affluence. Clarke accepted it as a reflection of what was important to them. It was not so much the house as it was the fact that they could afford to live in this upscale community.

He wanted to go straight to the bedroom that they called "his room" and hide, at least until dinner was served, but that was not an option. Taking an extra long time putting his things away was his futile attempt at postponing the inevitable.

Clarke knew he had not attained the status that his parents, especially his dad, had wanted for their only child. His father had never used the word "embarrassment," but the message was clear anyway. He dreaded the little digs and innuendos that would certainly come during his visit. Talking to his father was like being wrapped in barbed wire. It was never comfortable, and every attempt to move away from his father's topic of choice inflicted even more pain in an already uncomfortable situation.

The conversation with his father began with a list of recent happenings in their lives. A monologue would be a better description of his father's opening comments. He reported that they were members of a local country club and had recently taken up tennis.

Clarke amused himself with the thought of old people dressed in the latest tennis outfits. He didn't dare reveal his thoughts to his dad.

Wine tasting events were always on their agenda, and his father described in detail their latest purchases. Each wine had a unique and personal history that influenced its value to them. Bottles were arranged by their dollar value as an exhibition of their owner's financial success.

Several remodeling projects around the house made the bragging list. Clarke was satisfied to just listen. He secretly hoped his father would ramble on for hours.

His mom joined them in the den and jumped right in. "We are so glad you came. Christmas is a family time and we're glad you joined us."

Clarke felt obligated to respond with something polite. "Thanks, Mom. I appreciate the invitation."

"It has been a while," his father bluntly stated. Then he realized how harsh he sounded and offered, "It is good to have you around again."

"Do you have a girlfriend?" his mother pried.

"No, nothing serious to report," Clarke replied in hopes that there wouldn't be any more questions about his dating life. He didn't want to even think about it himself, much less to be cross-examined by his mother.

Fortunately, she moved on to another topic. She asked, "Did your father tell you we have taken up tennis?"

"Matter of fact, he did." Clarke didn't want to dwell on those thoughts and images again. Yet, he knew he could leave a moment of silence and one of them would move the conversation along.

His father didn't disappoint him. "We are concerned about the future of the economy. Things have been a little rough, but we manage," he said in a serious tone. "You know the mess the Republicans made of it, and it is going to take a while to set us on a positive course."

Clarke didn't know how to respond, so he didn't. Fortunately, his father was on a roll and kept right on harping on the GOP. "It is time to move beyond our arrogant, self-serving attitudes and join the rest of the civilized world."

His mom took the chance to escape back to the safety of the kitchen. She nodded as if she agreed as she rose from her seat and darted out of sight. Clarke was accustomed to abandonment, but he would leave if he could.

"Are you still working at the same job?" his dad asked in a feeble attempt to draw Clarke into the conversation.

"Yep," was his reply, followed by an awkward pause.

The expression on his father's face said it all—a mix of disdain and pity. Clarke knew his father would not endure silence very long and, as if on cue, his father spoke. "Well, at least you have a job. In this economy, I guess that's the best we can hope for." Years of experience had taught Clarke that this was just the first of many derogatory statements he would endure from his father's lips.

Fortunately, his father decided the conversation would move on to another subject. "The economic slowdown reminds me of the societal failure in South American countries where the masses are compelled to vote."

Clarke mentally checked out. He didn't care about the history lesson he was about to hear. He had heard it many times before. He knew the drill ... "dictatorships have their advantages" and "the masses need strong leadership that will take them where they need to go, rather than where they want to go."

Fortunately, his mother announced from the kitchen, "Gentlemen, dinner is served."

Her timing is impeccable, thought Clarke. She had interrupted before the history lesson was complete. Clarke, as a private rebellion against his father, quickly moved to the table before his father could complete another sentence.

Each place setting was immaculately arranged. "Pickard China is some of the finest ever made. It's American made, you know," his mom proudly stated. "I looked at one of the Pickard patterns they use at the White House, but I chose this one instead. Don't you just love it?"

Clarke lifted up the dinner plate and examined it carefully. Then he looked at his mom and smiled, "Mom, you have exquisite taste. You made an exceptional choice." He was so convincing that his mother thought his comment was genuine.

The food was very good. It gave the appearance of a home-cooked meal, but it all came prepackaged and ready to heat and eat. The hypocrisy was so evident. Everything on the table was the finest money could buy. The one really good part of his visit was the menu. Affluence does have its perks, and eating well was one he counted on. The food was always tasty and healthy.

Dinner conversation was lighter than usual. Clarke assumed it was just the influence of the holiday season. His parents were not religious, but they loved traditions, especially his mom. She viewed each part of Clarke's visit as some lifelong tradition, even when they were doing something for the first time.

After dinner, she served a light dessert. The dishes, as Clarke might have called them, were a special Christmas pattern china. He decided not to comment on his mom's description for fear that his sarcasm would not be disguised well enough. He did enjoy the dessert and told her so.

The evening passed without much more conversation, thanks to his mom's suggestion that they watch a Christmas movie together. Clarke accepted the idea as a perfect avoidance tactic.

They adjourned to the in-home theater room, where his father promptly dozed off. They spent the evening in silence as the movie played.

By the time the movie was over, it was bedtime. Clarke retreated to the safety and solitude of his bedroom. He hoped he could sleep most of the next day.

Chapter 18

Christmas Day, for Kent, was not much different than any other day off. Some might feel sorry for him and assume he was lonely, but that wasn't his sentiment at all. He actually enjoyed the solitude.

The day began with a simple breakfast, nothing special. The meal focused on fuel for his workout.

His daily routine customarily began much earlier, but this was Christmas Day. He allowed himself to sleep in as long as his body would tolerate. Seven a.m. seemed late, and he felt a twinge of guilt for his laziness.

The extra two hours of sleep had not been very restful. His thoughts continually turned to Helen. He knew this would be a difficult day for her. Efforts to put the thoughts out of his mind were initially futile. Helen and her family's situation dominated his thoughts.

He spent a good two and a half hours working out. Weight training and running were a regular defense against aging. Each day's battle was a small victory, but he knew he would never win the war. Like a good soldier, he would fight with every ounce of strength and never surrender.

Today's workout was strenuous. He poured himself into each rep in an effort to divert his focus away from Helen. He ran longer and farther than his typical workout. The tactic was only partially successful.

Life was not fair. David was dead, and his killer still roamed free. Kent felt an intense rage welling up inside him during his exercise. He wanted to find the man who had hurt Helen. He thought of several ways to deal with him, each and every one ending the same ... David's killer was dead. He deserved to die, and Kent would be glad to take care of it, personally.

The shower felt good. The warm water washed away the sweat and calmed the rage. Kent could feel the tension release. He followed his daily routine. Years of military service had formed routines and habits that remained intact, with almost no change. Structure seemed to provide its own special comfort. No day felt quite right without a morning dose of PT followed by a shower and shave. Holidays offered a reasonable excuse to skip the exercise, but he really enjoyed it.

His day would be filled with a variety of tasks. He didn't have any family and the corresponding obligations. His parents had died years ago, and he was an only child. His two failed marriages had not produced any children. He was alone for the day, or "free," as he liked to view it.

He did some writing for work and read several news articles on the computer. Lunch followed and consisted of a sandwich and fresh fruit.

His mind continually returned to thoughts of Helen. Their conversations played over and over in his head like an endless loop. He called her in the afternoon to wish her a Merry Christmas, but he intentionally kept it brief. Helen still dominated his thinking all day long. He would not yet admit, even to himself, that his feelings for her were steadily moving beyond friendship.

Late in the day, he spent time cleaning his pistol. He carefully took it apart to clean and check every piece. Each part was carefully inspected; then he reassembled each element with care.

He carried this gun regularly for personal protection. It also served as a signal to others, especially clients, of the seriousness of his work. He had grown very comfortable with a sidearm through years of military life. He also knew that gun ownership had been steadily increasing and had observed the impact on his clients.

Kent subconsciously knew that cleaning a weapon was like therapy. The feel of a gun in his hand was natural. It provided a unique kind of comfort that is only known to those who carry a weapon as part of their work attire. Like police officers, military personnel and others who protect the public every day, his weapon was part of his wardrobe. It was one more thing he put on as he dressed for work each day.

Security consulting had revealed that a license to carry a weapon, a concealed weapon, had risen sharply in recent years. Everyday citizens were arming themselves in increasing numbers, and the fact resulted in a double-edged sword. The reality that more and more people in any business environment carried a gun added a degree of deterrent to criminals. However, many of his clients were concerned about the possibility of workplace violence and sought his firm's expertise to mitigate the risks.

Murders, like David's, are just one reason some have sought a permit. Kent saw an increase in every sector of society. Women and men often armed themselves for personal protection. He wondered how many had actually thought about taking another life, even to protect their own.

For professionals like Kent, carrying is part of the job. He had taught handgun classes as a part of his military life. He emphasized safety as an important part of every class. Yet, he knew firsthand that there is a world of difference between paper targets and human beings. Taking another's life, even in war, changes you forever.

Chapter 19

Clarke was sound asleep when his mom knocked on his bedroom door. "Merry Christmas!" she announced with an irritatingly cheerful voice. "Are you hungry? Breakfast is ready."

He slowly realized where he was. He didn't want to get up, but he knew his mom would never leave him alone now. "I'll be there in a minute," he answered, wishing he had another option.

There was the warm, inviting aroma of coffee in the air. It filled the whole house. Fresh brewed coffee and other appetizing smells made the trek seem worth the effort, so he meandered toward the kitchen.

Clarke poured a mug and surveyed the morning menu. Breakfast would be a welcome shock to his body since his normal morning routine did not include nutrition of any sort. He was usually fortunate to have a vending machine snack by mid-morning.

The coffee was dark and delicious. Breakfast was a

mix of fruits and muffins. It was more food than any platoon of hungry soldiers could eat, but that was his mom's way. She supplied every possible muffin option in an effort to provide "just what her boy would want."

His dad was reading the newspaper as he did every morning. Christmas was no reason to break his routine. Coffee and a bran muffin with light butter were his staples.

The mood was not quite as tense as the previous evening. But Clarke did not want to push his luck. He quietly downed a couple of muffins while his mom led the conversation. She talked about their friends and several trips they had taken. She also gave an overview of the plans for the day. Opening gifts was on the morning agenda, the main event.

Then she gave a detailed account of the lunch menu. It would be, "the main meal of the day. Turkey with sausage stuffing, cranberry sauce, corn soufflé, green bean casserole, carrots, oven-baked potatoes and dinner rolls." Each item was what she thought Clarke would want. Then almost as an afterthought she added, "There will be pie a-la-mode for dessert."

"The afternoon would have some TV or movie time," she stated like a cruise director. Of course, those were actually code words for naptime. The plush leather recliners in the home-theater made perfect sense now.

Before she could continue, Clarke excused himself

and said, "I need to shower and get ready for the day."

"That would be nice," his father finally spoke. "Most people are up and dressed by now."

Clarke retreated to his room without responding. He took his time in the shower and getting dressed. Then he tinkered with email on his phone. He finally made his way down to the living room where the Christmas tree was located.

His mom looked up, "Oh, there you are. I was about to come check on you."

"Sorry, Mom, I got caught up in some emails on my phone."

"Oh, that's OK," she said cheerfully. "Let's exchange gifts now," as she patted the couch beside her to indicate where Clarke should sit.

He knew the signal and obliged her thinly veiled command. At least it placed her between him and his father.

She gave the first gift to Clarke and then folded her hands as if to say he should open it now. It was a shirt size box, expertly wrapped by someone paid to wrap gifts. Clarke opened the box and found a shirt and matching tie. The shirt was a light blue button down oxford with a classic yellow and blue silk tie.

He looked directly into his mother's eyes and said, "Thank you very much, Mom. These will knock'em out at my office." He omitted telling her his real thoughts—the shock of seeing him in a tie is what would knock 'em out.

She gave a wrapped box to his father next, and he opened it without comment. It was an overpriced watch, and he fastened it on his wrist immediately. "It fits perfectly," he said. "It will make a nice addition to my collection. I wanted one with royal blue accents. Thank you, my dear."

The next gift was a diamond tennis bracelet from his father to his mother. It was rather simple, but beautiful. His dad always had expensive taste. The gift was expensive and clearly spoke volumes about the giver. It was a bold statement about what he could afford to give and a gift for someone who already had everything she needed.

She put it on, as if to see if it fit. She held up her wrist to admire the sparkle. And it did sparkle in the Christmas lights. She looked at her husband and gave him a coy smile. Speaking softly, she said, "It is absolutely beautiful." Then she paused and exhaled a thoughtful sigh, "Thank you, honey."

She slipped off the bracelet and carefully fastened it back in its box. Every movement was slow and deliberate as if to cherish the moment a little longer.

Finally, she turned to Clarke and casually announced, "Your father has a gift for you too." She retrieved a small beautifully wrapped box from under the tree.

Clarke slowly unwrapped the box and set the bow, ribbon and foil paper to the side. He opened the box to reveal a $750 American Express gift card. His dad wanted to flaunt their wealth. At the same time, Clarke knew that the gift was intended to show his relative low estate in life. He looked forward to his online shopping spree with mixed feelings. He would enjoy buying things, but knew that a sting would be there too. His dad wanted him to make something important out of his life, and the tension was always there.

There were two identical boxes left under the tree. They were also professionally wrapped, marked with little tags that indicated one was for his father and the other for his mother.

A Christmas gift for each of his parents was one of the things he always dreaded. This year he lucked out and found something easy. He shopped online and came across a pair of plush monogrammed terrycloth bathrobes. When he saw the picture, he thought, Now there's a useless gift with an expensive, exclusive look. Then he said to himself, That's perfect for my folks. He was pleased with the price, mostly because they appeared to be far more expensive than they actually were. He ordered them gift-wrapped, of course.

His mom was thrilled. "The monogram," she commented, "shows how much thought went into your gift. Clarke, I love it."

Clarke smiled, "I'm glad you like it."

His father gave an approving nod, perhaps out of respect for his wife's feelings. He simply didn't speak.

She put her robe on over her clothes and wore it all morning. The gift made her day. She commented on it at least a dozen times as she paraded around the house.

Clarke was so glad she didn't know how little he actually paid and how little thought really went into his decision. He was thankful for Internet shopping and seventy-five percent off sales. He just kept his thoughts to himself as usual.

The day went by slowly. Much of it was spent in silence. The threesome seemed content with their own thoughts.

Fortunately for Clarke, his father was quiet and somber most of the day. At least he withheld his normal barrage of insults aimed at his son. After all, it was Christmas Day.

Christmas Day was finally over and Clarke was glad he would be headed home. His hope to endure a little less than 72 hours with minimal pain and suffering was all but realized.

Bagels and flavored cream cheese was the breakfast offering. His father was perched at the head of the table reading the morning paper. Clarke ate a bagel in silence as if he were afraid to wake an evil sleeping giant. His father seemed to be content in his own world, and Clarke didn't have any desire to open himself up to injury by engaging in conversation.

After a silent breakfast, he gathered his things for the ride to the airport. Both parents made the trip.

His mother could not endure silence, but her attempts at dialog were left hanging. She projected her own feelings on others and thought Clarke was just sad to be leaving so soon. In reality, he was glad the hours would soon be over.

At the curb, he retrieved his bag from the trunk. He gave his mother a hug and spoke softly to her. He nodded when she suggested he come back soon. "Maybe Easter weekend would be nice. The weather will be warmer, and spring is always a good time around here."

Clarke turned to his father and felt compelled to extend his hand. They stiffly shook hands, and then as if to take one parting shot, his father said, "You need a haircut son. Maybe you can do that before you come back."

Clarke quickly said, "Yes sir," and turned to walk away.

Before he reached the automatic doors he heard his father say to his mother and anyone else who might be listening, "Maybe he'll amount to something someday."

Clarke thought to himself, Maybe I will.

Chapter 20

New Year's Day was not a new beginning like Reggie hoped. He felt like a small, helpless animal, hunted and chased by a pack of hungry wolves. His imagination was his own worst enemy. Every sound in the hallway of his apartment building gave new life to images of police breaking down the door, with guns drawn, all pointed at him.

He knew he had to move. Running away seemed to be the only solution. Fret was draining life from him as if he were slowly bleeding to death. Escaping to somewhere far away would certainly help. He looked at a map and tried to picture a safe place. He would do any kind of work, but it needed to be a place large enough to hide in the crowd.

The greater Atlanta area seemed like the right place. He would begin again, hidden by the large number of people spread over a large area. He planned his move with care. He didn't want to leave a trail, and he didn't want to draw attention either.

He was fearful of creating suspicion, but he was more afraid of his own paranoia. At work, he gave two weeks notice and explained that he was moving to Florida to work for his cousin. He didn't have any relatives in Florida, but no one would ask any questions.

He gave no specifics to anyone and was careful to be vague enough to not leave a trail. He didn't own much, so he planned to travel light. He had pawned off everything of any size and prepared to move.

A name change would help, but he didn't know how. He did cancel his only credit card and went to an all cash lifestyle. He paid all his final bills. Escape, that's all he wanted.

He gassed up his car one last time, paid cash, and moved away. Everything he owned was packed in his car. He drove toward Atlanta in hopes of finding a new start, far from the troubles that waited just across the state line in Kansas.

Chapter 21

It was not a typical date, but the trip to the pistol range was as much about their growing relationship as it was about shooting. Helen wanted to become proficient with a handgun and that would have been reason enough. However, it was more than a fringe benefit that her teacher was Kent. His credentials were impeccable, of course, and his experience as a firearm instructor was first class. But she was interested in him long before she knew about his firearm credentials.

The range rented a variety of handguns as part of their services. This would offer her the opportunity to try out different styles and weights before she made a purchase.

He had chosen to begin with a .22 caliber handgun. It would be easy to handle and would not have much recoil. This would allow her to master the basics without the tiring effect of the kick of a more powerful weapon.

Kent was patient. This was too important to rush.

He planned for several sessions before she would be ready to decide on a personal firearm.

His objective was clear in his mind. He wanted her to master firearm safety first. That would be sufficient for this first trip. Other techniques could be tackled once she was comfortable with safety and the basics of handling a gun.

She was an attentive student as she closely listened to every word. Kent was not accustomed to students who maintained such consistent eye contact. It caused him to struggle a bit to return the gaze. There was also a hint of perfume in the air that distracted him from time to time.

This is serious business, he thought to himself. I can't allow myself to lose focus.

The safety lesson was complete. Before they moved on, he asked, "What is the most important thing you learned about firearm safety?"

After a brief pause, she stated, "Treat every gun as a loaded weapon."

"That's right. That's why the muzzle is always pointed downrange." She was ready, so he said, "Okay, now it's time to get comfortable with the weapon."

Kent attached a paper target to the clip on the chain and ran it about halfway down the range.

He explained that the objective was to hit the bull's-eye. He grinned at his own humor, and she looked back at him with a serious stare.

He laid the gun down on the counter in front of her. "Pick it up like this," as he demonstrated how to hold the gun. "Point it toward the target. And don't forget to breathe," there was a faint smile.

"This is a .22." he continued. "It doesn't have much kick and should be easy to handle. You will want to use a firm grip. In other words, hold on tight. I can assure you, it won't mind," he grinned again.

"Squeeze the trigger with a steady pressure. Don't pull, just squeeze. Your instinct may be to close your eyes, but don't. Look at the target, by way of the sites, until after the gun fires."

"You remember how to look at the target using the sights?"

She gave a simple, one word answer, "Yes."

"I'm going to fire off a few rounds so you can see and hear. Your ear protection will do its job, but it may seem loud, especially since we are indoors." He paused, and then looked at her, "Are you ready?"

She nodded an affirmative reply.

He turned his gaze downrange, pulled back the hammer and squeezed off three quick rounds. The paper target shook slightly, as if to shiver, when each bullet passed through. It didn't moved much, but it registered the impact and penetration.

When he was finished, he was actually impressed with his own accuracy. There was a nice group on the paper target. He carefully placed the hammer back to the safe position and laid down the gun. He retrieved the paper target. "That how it's done," he said as he admired his work.

He placed a new target in the clip and sent it downrange. "It's your turn. Don't worry about the first shot or two. Most people take a few rounds to get used to the feel of it." There was a brief pause. "Take your time. We've got all afternoon," he said with a smile.

She gave him a look that communicated his attempts at humor were tiresome. Then she grasped the pistol exactly as he had done. She pulled the hammer back into position and maintained her focus downrange, mimicking his every movement. She squeezed off three rounds, just as he had done, except for a longer pause between each shot. Then she replaced the hammer, laid the gun down and looked at him.

He peered at the paper target. He looked harder as if he was having trouble seeing, and then he retrieved the target. It moved toward them and arched as it traveled to within reach.

To his surprise, there was a group of three holes that could have been easily covered with a standard business card. His astonishment was evident. He looked at her, then back at the target.

Wow, he thought, that's some kind of beginner's

luck. He looked at her, smiled and said, "Nice shooting."

She responded with a slight smile, but no comment.

Kent looked at the target again, and then placed a new one on the clip. Once again, he placed it halfway down the range. He gave the simple instructions, "You did fine. Just do the same thing again."

She stepped up to the counter and repeated everything just as she had done the first time. Kent watched her even more closely this time. He noticed that she barely flinched as she fired each shot.

The results were similar. This time the grouping was not as tight, but a dollar bill would still easily cover all three.

He looked at her, sensing that this was not beginner's luck. His brow furrowed a bit as he asked, "Have you shot a pistol before?"

She looked at him with a tiny smile and responded with an obvious understatement, "A few times."

"Why didn't you say something?"

"You didn't ask," she said with a guilty shrug. "It has been a while, and I needed the review," she offered as a peace offering. "I did tell you I grew up on a farm. Guns were just a part of life. I have never had any training except from my dad."

"Well, he taught you well, my dear. You handle that pistol like a pro."

They spent time looking at and trying out different handguns. Kent had her try several different frames and sizes. They then worked with a couple of different calibers.

Helen chose a Glock G26 because of its small size. Kent told her the 9x19mm round was more than adequate. It just felt right in her hand, and it was easy to shoot.

Kent planned on adding a laser site. The additions would make it easier to use. He asked if the range rented any Glocks with a laser site attachment. They did not. Practice with that setup could wait until another time.

The day was more than he expected. Helen was everything an instructor could hope for. She handled herself with confidence and each firearm with care and respect.

Kent was surprised and could have been offended by her failure to inform him of her prior experience. He was not. Instead, he was proud that his girlfriend could handle a firearm.

Chapter 22

The office was simple, yet professional. Every detail communicated a commitment to quality. It was easy to tell that someone other than Kent had created the décor. This firm was a team that was very proficient at what they did and obviously hired other top professionals to do the work they did not have the expertise to undertake.

A stylishly dressed receptionist greeted Ray as he arrived for the interview. "Good afternoon. Welcome to Bree Security Consulting. How may I help you?"

"Good afternoon. My name is Ray Williams. I am here to see Mr. Bree."

"Mr. Williams, it is a pleasure to meet you. My name is Kayla." The voice came from his left, and as he looked toward the voice, he saw a woman moving toward him. Her attire was very professional and managed to disguise the extra pounds she carried.

"Mr. Bree is expecting you," continued Kayla.

"Would you like a cup of coffee, a soda or perhaps some bottled water?"

"No, thank you."

"Please follow me. Your meeting with Mr. Bree will begin in the conference room." She took a few steps down the hallway to the first door on the right. The door was already open. She turned and motioned for him to enter and followed him in.

A stylish wooden conference table was the centerpiece of the room. There were eight high-backed executive desk chairs symmetrically arranged around the table. A packet of information was positioned in front of the corner chair.

Kayla pointed to the packet and said, "This packet will give you an overview of our firm. If you have any questions, please let me know."

"Well, I see you've met the brains behind this operation," Kent said as he bounded into the conference room. "You probably thought I hired her for her looks, but she really does run this place. Kayla has the title 'office manager' and she keeps track of everything."

Ray's first thought was how different this office was from the place where he works now. There was a clear focus on quality, and yet a relaxed, professional atmosphere. His first impression was overwhelmingly positive.

"Let's have a seat and get started," Kent suggested.

Kent sat at the end of the table and gave a rather formal overview of the company. He ran through it just as he had done with each prospective client he had met with over the last several years. It was well presented, complete with a mission statement and all the rhetoric one would expect from the CEO.

"Do you have any questions so far?" Kent offered, to make the interview more conversational.

Ray asked, "What would you say is the product or service Bree provides to its client?"

"The product marketed by this firm is essentially a set of recommendations that will strengthen the client's defense against security threats," Kent summarized. "Our proposal includes companies or individuals the client might contract to implement each recommended action, but we seldom get involved in the implementation beyond some specialized training."

Kent described a typical client and how Bree approaches their needs. The conversation included considerable interaction, and Kent was pleased with Ray's comments and questions. He explained that the next part of the interview would involve the entire team. He suggested they take a short break before beginning the next phase.

After the break, Ray returned to the conference room. He looked through the paperwork that Kayla had alluded to earlier as he waited on the next part of the interview.

Each person introduced himself or herself as they entered the room. When they were all seated, there were six other people around the table. Kent asked each person to repeat his or her name and give an overview of his or her respective role on the team.

Kent asked, "Tony, how about getting us started?"

"My name is Antonio Jimenez, but I prefer 'Tony.' My contribution to the team is in the area of hardware solutions. My background includes work with video surveillance and camera systems, electronic access control systems, lighting and all things related. Although I also represent the team on information technology consultations, we usually outsource any network-related consult. Our goal is to provide an independent evaluation of their current systems and recommend any necessary or appropriate upgrades and additions."

"What he really means is he would really make a better crook than a consultant," another team member chided. "He can bypass any surveillance system and can hack most computer systems if you give him enough time. Tony usually adds several things to everyone's initial draft."

Tony just smiled in agreement and continued, "It is my job to look at the infrastructure and be certain we cover all the bases. I do that for every client, even when I am not the point person."

"Randy Higgins here. I specialize in personnel matters and staff training. For example, on a current project, our client is concerned about workplace violence, and on another I am addressing employee theft. Perhaps the most commonly overlooked personnel matter we find is the worker's sense of safety on the premises, especially if they have one or more parking decks. We outsource much of the personnel training we recommend, but I still provide some specialized training."

"I am Steve Pratt and I am the resident attorney. My area of specialization is legal matters. One important note is that Kayla and I are the only team members that are not former Army Special Forces. My main job is to keep us from losing our shirt in a major lawsuit. I review our recommendations to ensure we are not exposed to unnecessary legal risk. For our clients, I supplement what they already have in place. Our larger clients have legal counsel on retainer and do not require general legal advice. However, it never ceases to amaze me how many mid-sized companies don't have even the most basic legal documents. It makes my job easier and I look like a hero."

"Well my name is Hwan Chung, and I do as little as I can get away with. The company's website has me as the one who specializes in site security. What that usually means is parking lot and garage security. But I cover anything outside of the main buildings."

"He's our version of an inept cop who patrols the premises while everyone else works." Tony jested. "We don't let him inside very often. He can't seem to keep his hands off of everybody else's work."

Hwan shrugged as if to say, No comment.

"You already know me. I'm Kent Bree and I try my best to stay in front of these guys so I can claim to be the leader. My area is general risk assessment."

"What he's trying to say is, he's the boss," Hwan interrupted. "We have all agreed to let him live as if that's really true."

"Let me remind all of you, I sign your paycheck."

Kayla quietly added, "I co-sign all the checks to make sure they don't bounce."

"As I was saying ... I provide quasi leadership and general consulting. Much of my time is dedicated to the areas of international travel and living abroad. Many of our clients have personnel residing outside the U.S. I also participate as a volunteer in the orientation of students who are preparing for a semester or more of study abroad."

"Kayla, tell Ray how you keep us all out of trouble," added Kent, keeping things moving.

"Well, I check the spelling and grammar before we print and bind the written recommendation. These guys are smart, but let one of them create a new spelling for a word and the entire group will likely adopt the new spelling without question."

"Some people will just never let go, will they?" Steve commented, as if her dig was aimed at him more than the others.

Kayla continued, unfazed, "I research providers for everything we recommend and follow up with an evaluation of any work done based on our consultation. We are the client's advocate and want to be sure they are receiving quality work and service. You might say I work on service after the sale."

Kent began the wrap-up, "As you can see, all of our areas of expertise overlap to some degree and that is by design. That way we can leverage crosschecking within the team. Everyone is a generalist in the area of risk assessment, and to some degree, represents our firm to their particular client. However, everyone on the team reviews the written recommendations for every job.

"If you decide to join the team, your orientation will begin with the review of one completed project initiated by each team member. You will see the original version in Microsoft Word format with all the notes, comments and changes from each of the other team members. This collaborative version will give you a feel for how each one of us contributes to each project. An important dimension of our teamwork begins with a careful reading of each other's work.

"This written review is then followed by a team review here around this table. This may take some getting used to because we expect robust dialog. Recommendations to the client are vigorously scrutinized and even challenged. Kayla then produces a final written proposal.

"Our experience has found this to be a healthy process, but it does require a bit of practice. When ideas are examined this carefully, you must separate yourself from the concepts you present and be able to allow each component to be evaluated on its merits alone. We believe this process, as painful as it may be sometimes, results in a quality product for our client."

Kent continued, "You would bring a new dimension to the team. Your background and professional experience will contribute in the area of structures and construction in general. Does anyone have any questions?"

Ray had read up on the business before he arrived and asked a few relevant questions. Everyone, on both sides, felt the interview went very well.

Kent dismissed the others and invited Ray to stay. They talked a while and Kent made it clear that he thought Ray would be a good fit. He ended their meeting by offering Ray a position and told him to talk it over with Barbara and take all the time he needed to make a decision.

Ray left with mixed feelings. The new job would be a total change for him. He knew Kent and would enjoy working with him and for him. His mind raced, weighing all the pros and cons. The only thing he knew for sure was this would be a difficult decision.

Chapter 23

Clarke wanted to make his point. His views were his, and he was convinced, like most, that what he knew to be true was indeed true. He believed the facts were clear, even if others did not share his wisdom.

The facts, as he saw them, were undeniable. No argument could change the facts. The number one fact for him was simple: firearms kill. Guns are designed to kill, and no one will be safe until all guns are destroyed. He wanted to join with others to turn the tide, to make the world a safer place, but he was willing to go it alone if necessary.

Clarke's understanding of truth was not considered subjective. The formation of his deeply held beliefs about what is right and what is wrong occurred at a level deep within and resided somewhere in his subconscious. His deeply held beliefs were the foundation for every purposeful action.

Guns in the hands of police and military personnel were not part of Clarke's thought process. He employed a type of tunnel vision that excluded many otherwise logical considerations.

He believed that gun control required the elimination of all firearms. He detested what he observed in the gun control debate—that wherever the line is drawn, both sides always work to move the line. If assault weapons are prohibited, the gun control advocates will push for more control and the gun ownership advocates will strive to take back lost ground. The legal battles over guns are no longer about what is best for America. Guns, all guns, must go.

Clarke knew that when two vastly different worldviews collide, the result is conflict. His view of history was that wars have been fought over the centuries as one group sought to impose their views on others. The clash of opposing worldviews has been the root cause of most conflicts. To some, the debate over guns was nothing more than a turf war, but to Clarke, it was personal.

It all began as a conversation, not a dialog between people, but a conversation that existed only in Clarke's mind. The conversation sought to answer the question: What can be done to stop gun violence? At times the dialog was civil, but at others it was like a bitter war.

Clarke saw guns as a danger to the public. The NRA wielded too much power. It represented everything that was wrong with guns and gun ownership. Any mention of the NRA elicited a venomous internal rant in Clarke. He would silently denounce its unwarranted influence on lawmakers and the tragic results. He rehearsed in his mind his list of examples of the heartlessness of its supporters.

The solution for Clarke was simple. Guns needed to be gathered up and destroyed. The debate, the civil version, focused on convincing gun owners to turn in their weapons. If they could only see the truth, they would willingly join the movement to ban all guns. The less civil version sought means to prove his point.

Guns were evil. Stopping the violence perpetrated on the innocent was his noble calling. The end justified any means.

Another visit to a gun show was his logical next step. If they didn't learn the first time, he would give them another lesson.

Chapter 24

Clarke eased his car into the parking lot as if the combination of slow speed and careful driving would make him invisible. He was on enemy turf, and he did not want any contact with the other side. He parked between two pick-ups and wondered if his two-door eco-friendly car stood out as much as it seemed.

Weaving through the vehicles as he walked toward the entrance, he passed a pair of guys conducting their own business there in the parking lot. He was shocked to see a handgun being sold as if it were a box of Girl Scout cookies.

He stood in a short line and paid a few dollars for the entry fee. This was a much smaller show than the one he had disrupted near Atlanta. The drive took a little more than two hours to Warner Robins, Georgia. Located just a few miles south of Macon, it was not that far, but he sensed that this place was worlds apart from the northern suburbs of Atlanta that he called home.

There were two uniformed officers at the entrance, but they seemed to focus on their job of checking any guns that were being carried into the show. He drew in a deep breath as he walked passed them and made his way toward the first set of tables.

Guns were neatly arranged on each table. Most had a rubber-coated cable running through the finger guard of each firearm. This was a simple, but effective way to make them available for viewing and inspection, while at the same time keeping any of them from disappearing when the owner might be distracted.

Clarke scanned the room for a vantage point that would provide cover for his actions and also provide an escape route. This would be his only chance to scout out this two-day show. He would survey the area, finalize his plan, and return tomorrow to strike.

This show did not offer the advantages he had his first time around. He had visited the previous site several times for other events held in the same venue. He had deposited the duffle bag several days prior. He had reviewed his plan over and over again until he was certain that he had considered every possible contingency.

He couldn't help but notice that the clientele was not the same as the other show. There seemed to be a disproportionate number of what Clarke would call "rednecks." These were the epitome of what he saw as the uneducated societal misfits that made up the majority of rural America. His disdain for them flowed from somewhere deep within.

One noted exception was the military or law enforcement types. The haircuts were all similar and very short. There were several groups of them. He wondered if they were from Robins Air Force Base, located nearby in Warner Robins. Perhaps they were off-duty police officers. Regardless of who they were, Clarke made a mental note that they looked like the type who knew how to handle themselves. He guessed that they were very familiar with guns and would not be afraid to use them.

As he made his way past a table full of handguns, he overheard two of the rednecks talking. He observed them from a distance and listened carefully.

"Did you hear about the guy who shot-up the gun show up near Atlanta with a paintball gun?" the taller one asked with a singsong southern twang. His words captivated Clarke's attention as if someone had just pulled out a bullhorn and aimed it in his direction. He tuned in to hear the impact of his handiwork.

"Yep," responded his friend. "He must have been on something to pull a stunt like that. He must be absolutely crazy."

"Stupid is as stupid does!" the tall one said with a huge grin.

"No, I'm serious. What kind of person pulls out a

paintball gun on a crowd of people that are as armed and dangerous as a gun show crowd? You'd have to be absolutely nuts to do that."

"It was just a prank," as his grin began to drupe. "I don't think anybody even got hurt."

"Yeah, but that's the kind of prank that gets you shot dead. There may be a lot of places where you can pull a bone-headed stunt like that, but a room full of people buying and selling guns isn't the place."

"Well, one thing's for sure, he had better not try it again. The next time …"

Another group of people talking about the high price of the reloads at this show walked between them, and Clarke didn't hear the rest. He didn't need to; he'd heard enough.

The crowd moved deliberately. Conversations were generally louder than normal in order to be heard over the noise. Guns and ammo were the topic for most.

One tall, muscular man caught Clarke's attention. It wasn't anything he said. His sleeves were rolled up to reveal the tattoo of the Second Amendment that covered most of his right forearm. That's one way to advertise where you stand, thought Clarke. The words were permanently etched in his skin:

The Second Amendment

A well regulated militia,

> being necessary to
> the security of a free state,
> the right of the people
> to keep and bear arms,
> shall not be infringed.

This only confirmed Clarke's opinion. These are the kind of people who blindly "cling to their guns and their religion," as he once heard President Obama say.

Clarke felt superior to them. Their lack of social responsibility demonstrated their ignorance. They would respond with panic and run like wild animals when he unleashed his fury on them. He loathed them and their limited understanding of the world. They needed a lesson on the danger of the items on these tables. He would be their teacher. He would show them the error of their ways.

Clarke walked around the venue and looked at it from every angle. He thought about the way the crowd had responded in his previous experience. He was thrilled by the images as he replayed them in his mind. He searched for a similar vantage point, one that would allow him to orchestrate the same chaotic response.

This gun show area was not as large and the crowd was smaller too. He found a possible perch, but it was not raised enough. It offered little concealment. The military or law enforcement types flashed across his consciousness, and he knew he had to abort. This place just didn't feel right.

Unforeseen Impact

The decision to abort his plan was the right decision, yet he felt a deep nagging in his gut. These are the people that need a real lesson the most. There was no doubt in his mind, however, the situation demanded that he wait for another opportunity.

Walking around, like any other patron, seemed logical. He was more relaxed now that he knew this was not the right time and place. The pressure was off and the freedom filled him with a nervous energy.

A row of rifles neatly lined up along the backdrop caught his attention. He wondered what it would be like to fire one of these high-powered guns. Driven by impulse, he decided to amuse himself and pretend to shop for a rifle.

He approached one of the tables with his gaze fixed on the row of rifles leaning neatly in their place. The owner recognized his prey and began the seemingly innocent banter, "Looking for something in particular?"

The first words that crossed his mind seemed to escape like a reflex, "I'm looking for a rifle." Clarke almost flinched as he heard the words come out of his mouth.

"Well, you've come to the right place." The hook was set, he thought. Then he began to reel him in, "What ya got in mind?"

Clarke felt trapped at first, but he relaxed as he

thought about how ignorant the man sounded. He decided to play the game, have a little fun. He began with a half-truth, "I'm looking for something that can take a long shot, but doesn't have a lot of kick."

"What's your plan ... hunting or just targets?"

Hesitation gave a hint that he either didn't really have something in mind or maybe he was just a novice. The salesman played a hunch and decided there was nothing to lose by approaching him as an uninitiated gun buyer.

Before long, Clarke was the proud owner of a well-used Browning 243, with a cheep 3-9x40 scope. He paid cash and was glad that no information was exchanged. The price was much higher than it should have been for the condition, but it seemed right to Clarke. It was well below the original asking price and that was Clarke's only reference point. The salesman was glad to take his money.

Clarke had insisted on a case. He said it would be a deal breaker. Clarke wanted to conceal his purchase, and the need to protect it never even crossed his mind.

The salesman unloaded a canvas "case" made for a shotgun. It certainly didn't fit the gun. He knew it offered no real protection, but he praised it as a first-class carrying case. Clarke was on a role, and the salesman was glad to oblige him.

The scope was completely unprotected, and

carrying the gun in such a case would likely degrade the accuracy, but the salesman didn't care. Clarke had been an easy, willing victim. Both got what they wanted. Clarke sought concealment, and that was what he really cared about. For the seller, it was a case of here today and gone tomorrow. He took full advantage of an unsuspecting buyer.

Adrenaline gave Clarke a jolt of energy. He was excited and could hardly contain his enthusiasm. The purchase was unplanned and spontaneous. He was like a small child on Christmas morning. All he could think about was playing with his new toy. He told himself he was doing research, getting to know his enemy. He never saw the irony in his purchase. Yet, somewhere deep inside, he toyed with deadly ideas.

Chapter 25

Jennifer turned to her cameraman with enthusiasm and instructed him to follow her closely. They would be trolling for crazies in the crowd. He understood, without her actually saying anything, that their objective was to find some gun-loving lunatics who would rant about gun ownership and the Second Amendment.

Their goal was clear — they would construct a video montage that would demonstrate the fatal flaws in gun advocacy. The principle objective was to gather video evidence that would paint gun owners as poorly educated individuals with an abundance of ignorance. As a cameraman, he didn't care that much about the issues, but he loved the opportunity to display his creativity and ability to create a compelling video.

She reeled in her first catch with a simple question. He was a perfect fit with his disheveled look, old clothes and well-worn baseball style hat with the number "3" on the front. "Why are you here today?"

"I'm here looking for a new rifle. One with more knock-down power at a greater distance than the ones I have now."

"Why did you choose a gun show?" she baited, hoping for a reply that would coincide with her real objective.

"These shows have a great selection of rifles. I want to be able to compare my options side-by-side, and this show gives me that chance." His reply was potentially useful, but definitely not all she hoped for.

She snagged another willing candidate and asked the same simple question, "Tell me sir, why are you here at this gun show?"

"I'm just here to look around. I figure I might just find something I like."

"Have you ever been to a gun show before?" she inquired.

"Why sure!" he quipped. "Most everybody here has been to one of these before. They're a great place to get a bargain."

Jennifer saw that this interview wasn't going to be productive, so she continued her search for others. She shifted her approach and used a simple tactic to goad her victims to respond with more outrageous proclamations. She employed the rhetoric used by gun advocates to draw them in and then waited. She knew all the hot button issues and leveraged them to her advantage. The final version could be easily edited to make her seem objective.

In one moment she spoke of the Second Amendment like she was a faithful supporter and alluded to those who threatened it as the enemy. Once she had the attention of a prospective prey, she asked a loaded question, "What do you think of those who oppose the Second Amendment?"

One typical response was, "Anyone who is against the Second Amendment is not a patriot." Another was a simple affirmation of the right to bear arms as if everyone was already aware of the facts.

A woman chimed in with a reaction that was more suited to Jennifer's purpose. The woman began by saying, "Every citizen of this great country has the right to own and carry a weapon. It's the law." Then she added, "We have the right to protect ourselves from criminals and even from our own government if necessary."

The woman was not alone in her view, and Jennifer was well aware of that fact. There are proponents of the Second Amendment who firmly believe that it gives them the right to join in an armed rebellion against the U.S. government.

Jennifer, in an effort to provoke a more outlandish sound bite from this woman, egged her on by simply saying, "Do you feel like the government is too big and has too much power over the lives of its citizens?"

The woman lunged at the chance to lash out at the government. "Yes, I do! And we don't have to put up with it." She stared directly into the camera with a look that would convince anyone that she really meant business.

She continued, "The president has too much power. Those in the government are only interested in lining their pockets. Our taxes are ridiculously high already. The government is taking over everything. One day soon, when we have had enough, they are going to see the people revolt. It will be an armed revolt just like it was when we fought against the British. The American people will not stand for it."

Jennifer was pleased and hoped the video was capturing the venomous way this woman presented her point of view. She continued to ask a variety of questions. Each time she hoped to capture a more shocking assertion. The woman didn't disappoint her. She ended with a long, semi-coherent attack on everything wrong with "America."

Suddenly the interview turned really interesting when Jennifer asked a group of bystanders, "What do you think about the increasing epidemic of gun violence in America?"

A gentleman stepped out of the crowd and responded. "Well, the facts don't point to a general increase in gun deaths. The FBI reports that homicide rates have been stable or slightly declining for decades except for inner city teens.

Drug trafficking and gang violence account for the majority of the teenagers who die from guns. As a matter of fact, if you subtract the inner city numbers from America's homicide rates, our rates are lower than Britain's, where gun control laws have been in force for years. There really isn't an epidemic. Gun ownership is not the cause of violence in our cities; it is poverty, media violence and the decline of the family that are to blame."

The man was polite and articulate. He was not the typical attention-hungry bystander drawn to a news reporter and cameraman.

Jennifer thought to herself, That may be a great point for your side. Too bad it will be cut from the report. I will give the appearance of balance to appease the FCC, but you can bet that your best points will not get any air time. She fought back a smile as her thoughts went to the obvious—control over the content is a wonderful tool.

The man was obviously well prepared to defend gun ownership, but his next words hit a nerve. He touched the tender surface of the deep wound she fought so hard to hide from others. He brought up the topic of suicide.

He explained, "Gun bans do lower the gun suicide rates, but do not lower the actual rates of those taking their own life. Other means of suicide increase and the net effect is no change in the actual number of suicides. People who really want to kill themselves find a way. Gun control advocates often use suicide as a convenient argument for their cause without regard for the real impact on actual suicide rates."

His words angered Jennifer as the horrifying images of a dead teenager flooded her mind once again. Part of her wanted to lash out at him, to put him in his place, but the part that wanted to run from the images of the past was stronger.

She quickly turned to her cameraman and said, "I think we have enough." She immediately walked away, making her way back toward the news truck. Her mind was clear, this guy would be cut completely out of her report.

She was not herself the rest of the day. Her experience and preparation allowed her to push through the pain and finish the project. It was clearly not her best work, but it was adequate.

With the gun show tables in the background, they recorded an introduction and conclusion for the news. It would not be a live remote broadcast and only required a simple presentation. Jennifer used her computer gun control file to construct an assault on the gun show loophole. She sprinkled in a good dose of stats to demonstrate the deadly impact of guns in America's otherwise peaceful society.

Clarke walked by and overheard Jennifer's reporting. He hid his smile, but inside he was thrilled to hear some sanity in the mindsets of the chaos. He was behind enemy lines and he knew it. The voice of an ally was a welcome sound. He resisted the temptation to stop and listen and kept on walking.

He gently laid his new toy in the trunk, bounded to the driver's door and slid in behind the wheel.

Chapter 26

This seems easy enough, thought Clarke. He would simply follow the instructions he had seen on TV. He had repeatedly reviewed several recorded shows and memorized the sequence of steps for sighting in a rifle. He would simply follow the instructions exactly as they had been presented.

Clarke had discovered a series of television channels dedicated to guns. They were neatly grouped together by his cable provider. There were hours and hours of gun-related programming. Hunting seemed to get the most airtime. Handguns were often compared and their finer points discussed. Firearm manufacturers obviously contributed programming that showcased their latest addition to the market.

Clarke found the firearm education he wanted, but he hated every minute of it. His goal, as he told himself, was research. Knowing the enemy, that was all.

He was still nervous. He had never fired a rifle

before. His thoughts were mixed: How much kick will I feel from the rifle? This can't be that difficult. Have I gotten enough information from the video?

He checked the rifle again and switched off the safety. He looked through the scope and placed the crosshairs on the target. There was a bit of movement, and he subconsciously squeezed the rifle tighter. Then he mechanically reviewed the sequence of steps.

He drew in a deeper than normal breathe and exhaled about half the air he had inhaled and then stopped. He could hear his heart beating as he tried to focus on the target. He remembered that everything should be perfectly still and relaxed, but he was far from relaxed. He increased the pressure on the trigger. Suddenly, the rifle recoiled into his shoulder and the round made its way downrange. The powerful rush that came over him masked his shock.

He took a quick look through the scope to check and see exactly where he had hit the target. He never saw it. The thrill was enough. He had done exactly what the training video had prescribed and was sure he had hit the target dead center.

This type of exercise is repeated thousands of times each year by hunters looking forward to placing the crosshairs on an animal that would soon hang on their wall and by competitive shooters practicing for the next competition. Clarke's experience was different.

He was not a hunter sighting in his rifle; he was not preparing for a competition. It was just an exercise. He convinced himself that he was simply trying his hand at hitting a target from a distance.

Knowing your enemy and understanding his thinking are fundamental components in any good strategy. He didn't actually have a target in mind; he was just getting to know the enemy and understanding his thought patterns. Research, it was nothing more than research.

There was no harm in what he was doing. The battle raged in his mind, but it remained somewhere behind his conscious thoughts. Lurking like a lion waiting to pounce was the thought of putting the crosshairs on a person that represented all that is wrong with guns. All he knew was that he needed to teach them a lesson. Those ignorant, gun-toting defenders of the Second Amendment needed a lesson they would not soon forget.

The irony of his plans did not ever enter his mind. Using a gun to teach "them" a lesson was his logical conclusion. Blinded by his rage was perhaps one explanation. Whatever it was that took him from scare tactics with a paintball gun to contemplating the use of the lethal force of a .243 round was birthed somewhere deep inside where his emotions ruled. The logic was his and his alone. No one else would know. In fact, it was not yet a conscious thought in his own mind.

Chapter 27

Helen already knew what she wanted, thanks to their visits to the local pistol range. She was looking for a Glock G26. The small frame fit her hand, and it would be easy to carry in a purse.

Kent suggested they look at a pawnshop first and see what they could find. He knew they would probably have new and used firearms, but it was the relative privacy and personal service that was the real draw. He despised the big box stores with their huge open spaces and abundance of prying eyes, complete with video cameras. The smaller space and limited number of other clients was, by far, the better choice.

Helen didn't really want to shop. She knew what she wanted and was ready to make a purchase and move on. Nonetheless, she indulged Kent's desire to shop around and decided that this could be fun if she would allow herself.

The pawnshop owner was nothing like the guys on the TV shows. He was quiet, almost withdrawn. He was very attentive and waited on them as if he had all day.

The selection of small-framed handguns was extensive. Gun sales were up significantly in the wake of the recent highly publicized tragedies involving firearms. News coverage of such events always included gun control advocates and their desire to leverage the event to promote legislation to limit guns. The possibility of new anti-gun laws always produces a spike in gun sales. The sellers just followed the market demand and tried to anticipate the whims of an increasingly fickle public.

Kent was enjoying himself, and Helen began to have a good time too. She couldn't help thinking that these outings were just another excuse to spend time together. She smiled as she thought about their relationship.

Gun shopping was fun, and Kent loved every minute of it. He was like a child in a candy store. Each gun felt good in his hands. He worked the action of each with ease and proficiency.

Helen watched Kent with a combination of respect and admiration. It was obvious he knew guns. She was comforted by his expertise and trusted him now more than ever. His ability to sum up the pros and cons of each handgun gave her confidence in her own selection.

Kent inquired about a laser site for the Glock. There were a couple of options in stock, and Kent examined each very carefully.

He turned to Helen and asked her what she thought about the G26. She held it carefully in her hand and held it up so she could see down the sites. She handled it like a pro, and Kent was impressed and proud. She looked at it, worked the action and then looked back at Kent.

"It feels good in my hand. What do you think?"

Kent hesitated and then responded, "Your opinion is what counts. I would not hesitate to suggest a Glock. They make very reliable firearms."

"Let's do it," she said.

"I think a laser site will serve you well and significantly improve your accuracy in any stressful situation."

She appreciated his careful wording, but David's death flashed across her mind as she thought about the real reason for her purchase. She was not deterred at all, but the sting was still there.

She asked about the total, and Kent said it was a fair price. She left the pawnshop with her own pistol. The laser site was already attached.

Kent purchased a couple of boxes of ammunition as a "gift." He hoped they would spend the afternoon together at their favorite new hangout, the pistol range.

In the car, he looked into her eyes, smiled and said,

"You've got a fine weapon." He gave a long pause and then said, "I know that must have been difficult too."

She nodded agreement but didn't immediately respond. She stared at him for a long while, then she leaned over and gave him a brief kiss. Her emotions were mixed, but she wouldn't look away. Part of her felt the deep loss, yet the rest of her was drawn to this man. She sat up in her seat and looked out toward the road. Then she smiled and said, "Well, aren't we going to the range to try out my new gun?"

Kent laughed and simply said, "Sure!"

Chapter 28

He was hunting for a high value target in much the same way that a deer hunter might dedicate hours of work prior to opening day of hunting season in search of a trophy buck. He had long since moved away from gun shows, even though the images that still raged in his mind clamored for a response. This time it would be different, and he was determined to select both the target and the venue with care to ensure the maximum impact.

Clarke continued to search for the perfect opportunity to make his point. His plan was now very personal, and he wanted to lash out at the gun show crowd with a vengeance. He felt a driving need to prove that his efforts were not a hoax or a prank, yet he worked to force himself to use his analytical thinking to drive his judgment.

He had considered a wide range of tactics and had scoured the Internet for ideas and prospects. As he refined his plans, he became increasingly aware of the potential factors that might divert attention from his objective. Maintaining focus on his fundamental purpose was essential; however, the inner struggle raged on in a battle for his attention. Revenge was slowly, steadily gaining ground in its war against the ideology of gun control.

In his economy of scales, a high value target was measured by its relationship to the gun community. A confrontation had surfaced in his mind. He was questioning if another paintball attack was enough. Driven by revenge, he slowly began to try to rationalize the use of a gun. He thought, "You've got to fight fire with fire." The use of deadly force was under consideration, even though Clarke initially kept it in the realm of fantasy.

Potential venues were analyzed for ease of access and multiple exit options. Consideration was given to the general readiness of the venue's staff and clientele. This combination led him to look at a number of large, onetime gatherings and events. He specifically looked at events that provided little or no attention to safeguarding against armed attacks. A gun-free zone was a must. He was surprised at the number of these soft targets he found.

Several events were initially under consideration. One by one, he methodically went through his checklist and each time a relatively obscure men's meeting at a large church kept attracting his attention. It met all his criteria.

What first caught his attention was one of the speakers on the agenda. He was not even one of the main headliners for the event. It was the statement, "National Outdoor Rifle Champion," that first grabbed Clark's interest. It didn't matter that he was not even last year's winner of one of the many rifle competitions, but to Clarke he represented the perfect target.

A speaker at a church event was not in his initial search, but as he researched the event, it was an ideal fit. A low risk environment provided a high value candidate that would be unmistakably linked to the gun community.

It was no accident that Clarke would be drawn to the opportunity to make his point with a rifle champion. He had already rehearsed his statement to the crowd, "I chose him because he represents the lawless rampage of gun violence in America." He knew the media would be looking for a reason, and this time he wanted to leave no room for misinterpretation.

The men's meeting was perfect. A church event was an ideal soft target. He didn't have any personal experience with one of these supersized churches. In reality, he had no personal experience with any church of any size, but he felt certain that this type of event would not have armed security. He knew from his research that Georgia's law governing a license to carry a concealed weapon prohibits them in "houses of worship."

The event's schedule would allow him to survey the landscape on Friday evening and strike on Saturday. He would be like any other participant on the first day and simply abort if he found anything that would interfere with his plan.

Clarke would become a living legend, but would not be a martyr for his cause. He knew that if he were caught, he would not resist arrest. He was confident that, in the unlikely event that he was arrested, he would have the best legal counsel money could buy. He believed other gun control advocates would rally to his aid. He would be their hero.

Blood-red paintballs would instill the same level of panic he had witnessed before. It would also prove his point that the gun show attack was not a joke, not a hoax, and not a prank. It was a bold statement about the danger guns pose on American soil. His voice would be heard this time.

Chapter 29

"What's your pleasure?"

"Just the same will be fine," Reggie responded with a half smile. You would have to work at it not to like Henry. He thought.

Henry worked at making sure everybody had everything they needed. From hard to find auto parts to morning coffee, he was always, "Mister service with a smile."

"I'll be right back with a cup of strong black coffee."

"You don't have to do that," Reggie gently protested.

"I know I don't. But I want to," Henry said as he went out the door.

It was that way from the first day on this job. Reggie wasn't sure who Henry was at first. He just couldn't figure out this guy's angle. After about a month, he finally just accepted the fact that Henry had always been that way. Even the old timers agreed that he had always been way too happy.

He didn't know Henry's official title, but it was obvious that he kept things running. He certainly had earned everybody's respect and made assignments without coming across too strong. He was clearly in charge, but he just did it in such a way that made everybody feel important.

Reggie had found this job very quickly. The job interview was over almost as soon as it began. The owner could tell that he knew his way around a car engine and that was all he needed to know. No need to bother with references since job performance would soon tell him what he needed to know.

His work ethic was strong, not unlike his approach to breaking and entering. He was careful and thorough. Car repair came easy to him. He liked the predictability. Engines worked well when you did the work correctly, and there was a deep sense of satisfaction that came every time one roared to life again.

Life at work quickly became a place of escape. The friendly banter with other mechanics was a comforting distraction. He actually enjoyed the practical jokes that broke up the day. Lunch from a bag tasted good because it was shared with others rather than eaten alone.

No family or friends had been normal for him almost all his life. There were a few old memories, but they had long since faded into the past, too far away to touch him now.

It was the hours between work that gave new life to his personal demons. His real search was simple. Reggie yearned for absolution. He had caused the death of a fellow human being and it haunted him every minute of the day. Time alone was the worst of all.

He longed for freedom from guilt. A change in scenery didn't provide much relief. It eluded his grasp at every turn. His new residence was plagued by the same evil demons. There seemed to be no escape. Guilt hung over him like fog hanging in a mountain valley on cool mornings.

Living near Cartersville, Georgia, was a change. The sights and sounds were distinct and the surroundings were definitely different. He found the change invigorating at the start and went through the motions day by day with hope that things would be better with time.

Henry returned with his normal smile, coffee in hand, "Here's your coffee."

"Thanks."

"You have the oil change and tune-up of the red F-150 to finish, right?"

"Yes sir," came the southern-like reply that Reggie had already picked up from his new surroundings. "I'll be done in less than 30 minutes."

"Perfect. We promised it would be ready by 9:30 this morning. That will be well ahead of time. Let me know as soon as you finish."

"Sure thing," Reggie replied as he went to work.

He completed the job in less than 20 minutes and looked around for Henry. He saw him in the bay across from his. "The F-150 is ready. Do you want it up front?"

"That was quick," Henry responded. "Just park it up front, and I'll take care of it from there. The next job is to diagnose what's causing the 'odd noise' from the green Ford Taurus. All they said was, 'It's making an odd noise.' Let me know what you find."

"Okay, I'll see what 'odd noise' it's making."

The day passed quickly. Reggie liked his new job and really liked the people he worked with. His time at work gave new meaning to his days. He liked being busy. It kept his mind off his past and the haunting memories.

After work, Henry handed Reggie a one-page flyer about a men's meeting at a church. He glanced at the paper and thanked Henry. He folded it neatly and put it into his pocket.

When Reggie arrived home, he pulled the flyer out of his pocket. Henry had simply said, "Thought you might enjoy this event."

Reggie studied it carefully and recognized several

of the celebrities that would be speaking. At first he thought that this type of event just wasn't for him. He tossed it to the side and decided not to think about it anymore.

Chapter 30

Initial meetings with potential clients were usually all about marketing and sales. This would be different.

Business success had put Kent in unfamiliar territory. Referrals kept his firm busy and there was little need to focus time drumming up business. In the beginning, the firm had been like most new business ventures, heavily invested in client development. Thanks, in part, to the extensive media attention focused on workplace violence, coupled with an increase in genuine threats, business was booming. Their workload could continue to grow based on referrals alone.

The team constantly worked to generate new clients, keeping an eye toward expansion into new arenas. The security business was healthy, and the team was well established in their field.

This led Kent to pursue a select number of clients with a more philanthropic attitude. His objective was twofold. He wanted to provide services to clients who could not normally invest in the level of professional services Bree Consulting offered, but he also wanted to explore emerging possibilities.

This meeting was with one of those potential clients. The need had come to his attention through the CEO of an existing client. He was very active in leadership at his church. He asked Kent to meet with the leadership team at the church and provide some pro bono consulting. Kent had accepted immediately.

The meeting began in a fashion that caught him completely off guard. Prayer was the first item on the agenda. Kent reached way back into his past memories and politely bowed his head and closed his eyes. The prayer was brief and included a request that Kent and his business be blessed. He was not expecting a prayer and certainly did not expect to be the subject.

Each attendee was quickly introduced. The senior pastor was well known, and Kent considered him a celebrity. Any public figure with the level of name, face, and, in his case, voice recognition could certainly benefit from a security review. The other four were senior staff and each held a key leadership position.

The next item on the agenda was an overview of the church's activities and events. Words and phrases were used that Kent had not heard in years. There were worship services, several each weekend. These were by far the largest regular activities. There were other events throughout the week and each was identified by age-range and average number of participants. Events ranged from seasonal sporting events to small group Bible studies. An assortment of banquets and other meals were also included. There were weddings and funerals for the average church members and assorted dignitaries. They also hosted large one-time events, and an upcoming men's meeting was used as an example. The organization of this complex mix of events and activities was impressive.

Another individual presented a multipage staff organizational diagram. Senior staff leaders were responsible for personnel and all programs in their areas. The total number of paid staff was also provided for each section. At the end of the presentation, the total full-time staff was announced as 122, with an additional 78 part-time paid staff. The number of volunteer leaders was also given with the note that this number fluctuated seasonally.

Al was the chief administrator for the church. He was obviously the senior pastor's second in command. His demeanor was humble, but there was no question that he was well respected and clearly in charge. He handled the meeting with efficiency and professionalism. Kent was curious about his background and guessed he had been recruited from a top business background.

The agenda provided Kent an opportunity to present an overview of his firm's work. He began, as he often did, by stating, "A team approach is our greatest strength. We provide individual service, tailored to each client's unique needs."

The overview included other elements, and Kent provided relative examples. He adapted his regular presentation to accommodate the unique situations of a church. It went well, and he felt good about how the group received it. He paid close attention to the way the individuals reacted and made adjustments on the fly.

Al smoothly transitioned into the next agenda item, a Q&A time. The first question was posed by one of the senior staff. He asked, "How would you assist an organization like ours?"

"To be completely transparent, we have never consulted a church before. However, our team approach leverages a wide range of skills and experience. Our 'product' is a comprehensive plan and assistance with the implementation of that plan."

After a brief pause, he continued, "We have consulted with several universities and educational institutions, which will serve us well on your multi-function campus. Experience with security for large conventions and board meetings will provide valuable insight for addressing the events you have that involve a large number in attendance. We also bring extensive experience with building and parking lot security. But experience has its limits, and our greatest strength is our ability to assist your team in the planning and implementation of comprehensive strategies that leverage technology and equip your personnel to limit risks while preparing to respond to emergencies."

Another question was posed by the senior pastor, "What emergencies do we prepare for and how?"

"Redundancy and contingency planning are often the keys to an effective emergency response plan," started Kent. "The objective is to prepare for emergencies by categories. For example, the simple step of contacting the appropriate first responders should be well planned to include every possible contingency and then appropriate levels of redundancy."

Kent looked around the table and could see that everyone wanted more information. He continued, "Who will call? and Who will they call? are important questions to ask in advance. History demonstrates, however, the need to go beyond these initial questions and design a matrix or web of responsible people who know the standard 911 number, but also know the direct phone numbers to the 911 office, police, fire and EMTs. As a contingency, what should be done if cell phones are overwhelmed? Who will direct the first responders to the proper location on such an expansive campus?"

There was an audible sigh from one of the participants.

"Bree Consulting provides experience and

knowledge to address these complex issues. We will review your current plans and processes. Our goal is to assist your team in evaluating each area and to develop an implementation plan."

There were a few other questions, and Kent expertly shortened his responses to each.

The initial meeting went very well. Al summed up the meeting and identified the action items. He delegated assignments to the staff with instructions for how and when to report.

They agreed that Kent's firm needed to observe their larger activities firsthand to adequately grasp the scope and diversity of their regular and special events. Al would handle the coordination.

The meeting adjourned punctually as indicated. Kent was cordially greeted by each attendee and had a brief conversation with each. The senior pastor was first, and Kent was impressed by his comments. He had listened well, and his grasp of the overview was evident.

Al was the last to shake Kent's hand. He inquired if Kent had time for a campus tour. Kent responded affirmatively, and they left together.

Chapter 31

The follow-up lunch was Kent's suggestion, and Al was pleased to have more time with him. He understood the use of a meal to conduct business, and he welcomed the opportunity.

The initial conversation revolved around the security review of the church and its programs. Kent continued to ask questions to assist his team in exceeding the client's needs and expectations. Information was a valuable resource, but the client's perspective was even more important. Al was the obvious decision maker, and his views would be an important key.

Al also asked insightful questions. He was certainly accustomed to dealing with high-level negotiations and decisions. He earned Kent's respect with his ability to represent the church with transparency and honesty concerning their level of preparedness while maintaining a strong negotiating position.

Together they agreed on the scope of Bree's security review. They discussed the priorities among the elements to be addressed.

Kent suggested a private consultation with the senior pastor to address his personal security in light of his public notoriety. He indicated there were some simple precautions that would significantly improve his safety without hindering his public availability and approachability. Al knew Kent's awareness of his boss's public image would resonate with the senior pastor.

The relative informality of their conversation provided an opportunity for Kent to mention the inclusion of a prospective team member in the consultation. He did not mention Ray by name, but made sure that Al was informed and in agreement. Kent wanted to give Ray a taste of their work, and this project would be an ideal real-world opportunity.

As the meal progressed, the conversation gradually turned away from business and began to touch on more personal issues. They shared a growing mutual respect, and the topics included their backgrounds and experiences.

Kent mentioned his military career and how it provided the expertise for his current role. He also mentioned how those years had introduced him to all but one of his current team members. This allowed him to point out their credentials and his firsthand knowledge of their integrity and work ethic.

As they continued, Al talked openly about his faith

in God. He described his childhood and the lack of any spiritual guidance during his early years. An advanced degree in business from Yale led to a successful career, but led him away from God and religion. He told how God intervened in his life and changed his priorities completely.

Kent found Al's story interesting, even strangely appealing. He had seldom met anyone like Al. The respect he had for him was only increased by their conversation. Religion was usually a dead-end for Kent, but Al was different.

Southern hospitality was something Al liked about his job at the church. He had been raised in a poor neighborhood near the downtown district of a city up north. There was a genuine concern for others in this church, not something he had known in his childhood.

The topics continued to vary, but all seemed to revolve around their personal history. Al started to talk about a topic that had always elicited a strong response from him. Perhaps it was a sign that he was a bit too comfortable with Kent. Yet, it was Al who first mentioned gun control.

Kent had strong personal opinions about guns, but he had a growing respect for Al and welcomed his perspective. Al began by expressing his reservations about guns in general. Kent would normally have been mentally defensive, but he genuinely wanted to hear Al's concerns and listened carefully. Perhaps for the first time, he really listened to other views on guns and gun control.

Al wasn't thinking about the relationship of his comments to the security consultation; he was just talking about current events. He began with a rather rhetorical observation. "Guns and gun control are in the news these days," he started. "I think there are plenty of guns already. I think we need better gun control."

"What would you propose?" Kent asked, hoping to get some clear signal and insight from Al.

Al glanced away, as if he were not speaking to anyone in particular, and said, "I think we need to make it really difficult for criminals to acquire guns. The real problem with guns is they end up in the wrong hands."

Kent wasn't sure where this was going. He agreed that guns in the hands of criminals are a problem, but he felt there must be more to this. He simply waited.

Al continued, "Gun buy-back programs, aimed at getting guns off the street, are a useful first step. Such measures decrease the availability of guns and ultimately save lives."

"Gun-free zones help provide a margin of safety around select locations. Adding other gun-free zones will help reduce violence," he continued. "Georgia has a law that makes all churches, or 'houses of worship,' gun-free zones. That's a good example. Churches are for worship and prayer, not a place for guns."

He was on a roll now, and Kent just listened. "Laws are needed that limit the capacity of magazines, especially for semiautomatic weapons. The 10-round limit seems to provide a logical margin of safety for the public."

"Closing the gun show loophole that allows gun sales without background checks makes perfect sense. Background checks reduce the availability of guns to criminals."

"A ban on the sale of assault weapons would increase public safety. Who needs a machine gun? They are not for non-military use. They pose a danger to other citizens and have no legitimate value to the owner."

There was a long, uncomfortable silence. Al realized he had just completed an aggressive, augmentative monologue. He believed everything he had said, yet he regretted the timing. It had come out of nowhere, and he was surprised by his own words.

Al apologized, "Please don't take my comments as a negative reflection on you or your team. I really am sorry," he paused. "I shouldn't have mentioned my personal views on the gun control debate. I'll be the first to admit that my views are not shared by a majority of our church members. This is Georgia and that tells you a lot about our constituency."

Kent was relieved, but still a bit perplexed. Al was clearly a professional, and his actions were unexpected. Yet, he had seldom heard someone give such clear arguments. The situation seemed to demand a response, so he said, "Thank you for your transparency. I am grateful that you mentioned your concerns. I may not agree with you on some of these issues, but I respect you enough that I'm glad to hear your point of view."

His relative loss of composure bothered Al. He viewed his actions as unprofessional, at best. Yet, these were his sincere beliefs and they were not intended to be vindictive or harsh. He felt a mixture of regret and relief.

The remainder of their lunch continued on other topics. Kent was not offended; he did make a mental note to tread lightly on any issue dealing with guns.

Chapter 32

The offer from Kent was more than fair. Ray wanted to take the job; however, it would be a drastic career change and would alter everything about his life.

Barbara was supportive. She thought the change would be good for her husband. She knew Kent and the long, special relationship the two men had over many years.

On one hand, Ray was attracted to the adventure. On the other, he knew he was safe in his current position and he was held back by the desire to stay in his comfort zone. He was appreciative that Kent told him to take the time he needed to consider the offer, but he knew he needed to give him an answer.

Kent had invited Ray to participate in a project as an additional step in the process. He also felt it would be the best way for Ray to be sure of his decision. Ray agreed and welcomed the opportunity.

The church client was an ideal starting point for Ray. The unique mix of building styles and construction spanned decades of building codes. The buildings were used for every type of public and private gathering. Some buildings were designed for large audiences. Some had flexible designs. The one thing they all seemed to have in common was that little thought was given to security. In most cases, it was an afterthought at best.

Ray carefully reviewed each building on the campus map. The packet that Kayla had prepared from Kent's initial meeting with the leadership team was divided into two sections: (1) items from the initial meeting and (2) items Kayla had gathered from other sources.

Ray digested the information like a college student studying for his first week of exams. He wanted to know as much as he could before he stepped foot on the site.

The "Chapel," as it was labeled on the map, appeared to be a renovated version of the original church. Kayla had found a number of pictures from a wedding brochure she located online. It seemed to be the oldest construction.

The "Worship Center" was the newest addition and included the latest technology in just about every category. A building layout, designed for new attendees, provided both the layout and the primary use of each room. There were several rooms behind the stage area that had labels like:

choir suite, orchestra suite, prayer room, and baptismal suite. The main worship area was large and was divided into sections by wide aisles. Video cameras on elevated platforms dotted the room. The balcony included a section marked "video and audio." This was a large area which included several rooms.

Ray realized that this building alone was going to be a security challenge. He made several notes about areas he needed to see firsthand.

An opportunity to study the layout would be invaluable to him on his first field visit. Kent had suggested that Ray might attend the men's meeting to see how the facilities look during a well-attended event. Ray agreed. Kent would be returning to Atlanta on a flight early that Saturday. He would come straight there from the airport. They would meet at the church and talk about the project.

Chapter 33

She opened the mailbox and retrieved her mail. Amid the clutter of pizza ads and other junk mail was an official looking envelope from the county. Helen opened it carefully.

It had been over a month since she completed the paperwork, fingerprinting, and background check, and filed everything with the authorities. But, there it was. Her permit to carry a concealed weapon had finally arrived.

Kent had walked her through the process, step-by-step. She had asked him several questions about personal protection. Their conversations had led to several trips to the pistol range and, ultimately, to her application for the permit.

She wondered what her students would think about her gun purchase. Their math teacher owned a handgun and was a fair marksman. Would her students be surprised? Would they approve? Some would and others probably wouldn't, but that didn't matter anymore.

Memories flooded her conscience and caused her to stop in her tracks. David was dead because of a gun. The hurt ran deep. Her emotions were still raw and tender. Life would forever be punctuated by his untimely death.

She wanted to live in a way that honored his life. Preparation was an integral part of that life statement. She would not be a victim. She would not live in fear. She would not allow another criminal to rob her of the precious life she now had.

Kent was her rock, the man she needed. He filled a void in her life that had been there for years. Since her divorce, she had wanted someone to share life with, but she had not actively searched. He had miraculously appeared across the room at a Christmas party.

Time revealed how each had considered not even going to the event that had changed both of their lives. It was fate, some would say. Others might call it luck, good fortune or destiny; it didn't matter now.

Life had new joy because she shared it with this man. He had been there during the most difficult challenge she had ever faced. Death had invaded and, somehow, he had softened the blow.

Now, she was ready to face any threat. Being armed was only part of her readiness. The capability to hit any target with accuracy was equally integral. She was prepared to carry her Glock, licensed to conceal it from prying eyes. She was prepared and ready to use it to defend herself and those around her.

His phone rang and an image of Helen appeared on the screen. He answered, "Hello, good to hear from you."

"Just wanted you to know that my permit arrived in the mail today."

"Congratulations!"

"Why, thank you. I plan to carry my new gun with me all the time and keep it close at hand, especially at home," she declared. "I know you are at work, so I'll let you go."

"I'll see you later."

She loaded the clip with 10 rounds and slid it into the handle until it clicked into place. She gently placed the gun in her purse. This simple action was the completion of a long road, an extremely emotional pathway. Her resolve was strong, and her conscience was clear. She was ready.

Chapter 34

The Friday of the men's event started like most Fridays. Henry was his usual friendly self. He didn't pressure anyone to attend, but he made sure to mention the meeting to everyone in the shop.

Reggie had not thought about it since the day Henry had given him the flyer. He had wondered what it would be like, but had not given it much thought.

Mid-morning, Henry stopped by Reggie's bay and asked how the job was going. This would probably be viewed by some as "the boss checking-up on you," but it never seemed that way with Henry. He occasionally offered helpful advice, but mostly just made sure you had everything you needed to complete the job. Reggie liked his visits. They were always brief and made Henry seem more like a helpful big brother than the boss.

Henry caught Reggie a bit off guard when he asked, "Did you bring your lunch today?"

"No," he answered, "I'll just grab a burger across

the street."

"Can I buy your lunch today?"

Reggie tried to quickly think of what he might have done wrong, but nothing came to mind. "Sure." There was a hint of caution in his voice.

"Don't worry. I just want a chance to talk. There's no problem or anything."

The words were comforting to Reggie, but his curiosity was running on high octane.

Henry turned to walk away and said, "I'll be back at about 12:15."

Reggie continued his work, but his mind couldn't shake the lunch invitation. He thought about what it might mean as he continued working.

Twelve fifteen finally came and Henry was right on time. "I hope you like Mexican food."

"That sounds great to me," Reggie said with a smile.

Chips and salsa were on the table as soon as they sat down. Henry said, "Reggie, I want you to know that I think you're doing a great job. Your work is always well done, and I appreciate your dedication."

Reggie could feel the tension release from his body. It was as if someone had just released the valve on a tire. He hoped it wasn't as visible as what he felt.

Unforeseen Impact

"I have two reasons for inviting you to lunch," he said as he scooped up a chip full of salsa. "First, I wanted the chance to tell you how well you are doing. The other reason is personal. I hope you don't mind."

"No, not at all," Reggie grabbed a chip and dipped it into the bowl. Unlike Henry, he held the chip so the salsa would run off before he tossed it into his mouth.

The server took their orders; both ordered from the lunch specials. Chips and salsa were going fast as they both enjoyed the appetizer.

Henry began to talk about his faith in God. He articulated very succinctly how he came to understand his need to change and become a follower of Jesus. His life had been very different since that day. "Living for Jesus" was how he phrased it. Everything about his life was framed by his decision to live for Christ.

Reggie felt the sincerity in Henry's words, and he could not escape their impact. Henry had lived his daily life of joy out in the open for everyone to see. It gave his words power and impact.

Henry was not pushy or insistent. He didn't belabor his message. He had said enough to Reggie, and he left any response up to him.

Reggie didn't want to respond to Henry about God, so he moved the conversation back to work. It was a safe subject. "What jobs will we be working on this afternoon?"

Henry gave a simple, direct answer, "We have three tune-ups, two brake jobs, several diagnostic jobs, and a new set of tires on a sedan. Do you have a preference?"

"Not really. I'll do whatever you need done," was his genuine reply.

The server placed their selections on the table in front of each man. The food was delicious and the dialogue continued as they ate.

"Work has been good lately, and fortunately, we have plenty to do," Henry observed.

"Well, we sure seem to stay busy."

Henry didn't reply. He simply allowed the silence to hang in the air.

Reggie tried to think of a topic to break the silence. "You seem to really have a handle on this God thing," hoping that Henry would talk a while.

Henry chuckled a little and said, "Well, I've never thought of it that way. I just know that God really does love me, even when I mess up."

"That's when He punishes you, right?"

"Not exactly," Henry said thoughtfully. "Not if I truly regret what I've done and ask for His forgiveness. God wants to forgive me, but I have to want it too."

Finally, Reggie asked the question that was always on his mind. "Do you think God will forgive someone who really messes up?"

"Sure," came Henry's confident reply. "Like I said, God wants to forgive. He can and will forgive anybody, regardless of what they've done."

The conversation paused while both men ate. Reggie thought about what Henry had said. He dared not say what was really on his mind, *God would never forgive me. I killed a man. Henry would never understand a guy like me.*

In time, Henry paid the bill and left a generous tip. They returned to work like longtime friends.

Chapter 35

The meeting had been on the calendar for more than a year. It was now only a few hours away and everything had been checked and rechecked. The planning committee had arranged for an impressive list of speakers that most men, evangelical Christian or not, would recognize. They deeply believed that God had blessed their efforts to create an event like this.

It would be a meeting for men. There would be two days, beginning with Friday evening and continuing all day on Saturday. The schedule featured a top baseball player, a successful college football coach, the CEO of a Fortune 500 company, and other leaders that men respected and wanted to hear. It was an impressive list of celebrities for any meeting, but remarkably exciting for an event hosted by an individual church, even if it was what some in the church business call a mega-church.

The venue would seat more than two thousand and was expected to be full when the top speakers addressed the crowd. It would be nondenominational, said the advertisement, drawing evangelical Christian men from all walks of life. This event promised to provide something meaningful for every man.

It was late Friday afternoon, and men had been gathering for hours. The atmosphere was filled with excitement and expectation. The organizers expected this to be a meeting to remember. They had no idea that other plans had been made to make this a gathering that would catapult it into the national headlines.

Worship music by a rock-sounding band filled the air, signaling that the launch was near. Events like this provide a nonstop flow of inspirational music and speakers. Yet, Clarke was present for an entirely different purpose. He was going to strike his blow to the very heart of the gun community. This Friday night session would give him one last chance to review everything, and if necessary, one last chance to abort.

As always, he planned his work carefully. He had visited the church on a busy Sunday to search for an appropriate vantage point. There were several options. The high spots offered limited escape options, but provided excellent views. The best seemed to be the simple option. A low location near the front would offer an unobstructed view of the stage and open views of large sections of the crowd. The aisles they would enter would act like a funnel, and, of course, a variety of escape routes for him.

He walked through several of these and decided on his order of preference. Alternatives and options were key to success. His planning was focused and thorough. He didn't want to leave anything to chance. This was going to be the answer he had searched for and his chance to change the course of history.

Reggie hated weekends, especially when he had Saturday off. It gave him too much time alone. He often chose one of several ways to escape from reality. A bar, with drinks to dull the senses, was the usual choice.

When he arrived home, he saw the flyer and remembered Henry's invitation. Several of the men on the schedule were famous. He decided to give it a try. He could always leave early if he didn't like what was going on.

A quick shower and he was on his way. He struggled with his decision and almost turned around several times. The desire to not be alone finally won and he arrived at the expansive campus. There were plenty of men helping traffic flow through the parking lots. He followed the direction of the orange cones and flashlights and parked as directed.

He was greeted by several men as they guided the arriving masses through the maze of parked cars and moved them toward the main building. Reggie was met by other men just outside the building. They welcomed him, shook his hand, and offered helpful information and directions.

His first impressions were positive, almost overwhelming. The men were not dressed in suits and ties. They were dressed in team jerseys, camo jackets, and other attire that regular people wear. They were friendly and seemed genuine in their desire to help. Reggie's doubts about this experience began to subside with each encounter.

Clarke checked for security personnel as he wandered around the main building and found none. There were two police officers directing traffic, one at each main parking lot entrance/exit on the main road. He assumed the same number would be at the exits at the dismissal time on Saturday. It really didn't matter since his exit plan had already accounted for them. He did not find any armed personnel on the premises.

The meeting area was the church's main worship center. A steeply slanted floor gave everyone an unobstructed view of the platform. The seating was arranged in large semicircles or arcs that wrapped around the platform area. This shortened the distance between the speaker and the crowd; even those in the last rows on the main floor, as well as those in the balcony, seemed close to the main speaker.

The platform was large and could have easily accommodated a full-scale theatrical performance. However, each speaker would use the small stand that literally placed him front and center. Two massive screens carried live images of the speakers and gave an intimate feel that defied the size of the gathering. It was impressive for anyone, but especially those who seldom, if ever, had attended a church service.

Clarke walked through the corridors outside the main meeting room during one of the top name speakers for the evening. The hallways were virtually empty. There was one gentleman hurriedly making his way to and from the restroom. Yet, there was not a single person standing around outside the main auditorium. There were no security cameras in the hallways, nothing that would prevent him from going through with his plan.

Clarke saw no reason to abort; the plan was a go. He exited the building and made his way to his car. He had seen everything he needed to see and wanted to leave before the crowd.

Reggie was having a good time. It was a welcome surprise. The people around him were "normal" and not at all what he expected. The speakers were all well-known celebrities. Many were funny, and it seemed like entertainment and not preaching. He was impressed with how genuine they all seemed.

He decided he needed to arrive early the next morning in order to get a better seat. His decision to sit in the back section of the balcony had been strategic, in case he needed to leave, but now he wished he'd moved a little closer.

Time passed quickly and it was already after 10:00 p.m. He was hooked and was glad Henry had invited him. He'd looked for Henry, but the crowd was way too big. Maybe tomorrow, he thought. If not, he would see him on Monday.

Chapter 36

Saturday morning came quickly. The weather was just what the organizers had asked for, blue skies with a few puffy white clouds. No rain, just a beautiful day. Cool, but not cold for early March.

The mood was festive, as if those arriving were going to a ballgame or other big sporting event. There were men of all ages gathering for more worship and inspiration. Men arrived in groups, large and small. One threesome appeared to be three generations of the same family. There were larger groups that trickled through the parked cars on their way in from church buses lining up along the outer edge of the parking lot. Plenty more men arrived, one to a vehicle.

Ray had arrived along with the other early birds. He parked in the first row behind the handicap parking area and watched for a while from his pick-up. He took a few notes and continued to work as if he had already taken the job at Bree Consulting. He spent much of his time just people watching. He hoped that Kent's flight was not delayed and they would have plenty of time to walk the campus together. This would be a real scenario designed to give Ray an accurate understanding of what the job would be like. It would also give Kent an introduction to a megachurch in action.

Time passed slowly for Ray. It wasn't boredom, but the time seemed to drag as he watched men of every shape and size move across the blacktop. There was plenty of variety. They arrived in different types of vehicles, some in four-by-four pick-ups, others in luxury sedans, and every variation in between. Their clothing ranged from a few suits and ties, to shorts and flip-flops. The assortment was actually quite remarkable. The event was living up to its advertisement.

Ray pondered the idea of Who didn't fit? Perhaps a woman would be out of the norm, but as he watched them filing by, he couldn't imagine any man who would not be welcome. It became a sort of mental game. He conjured up a variety of images: first a homeless man, then a group of homeless men, then a drug addict, then some gang members, then some rowdy party crashers …

That's when it hit him. These images were the former lives, not just of the attendees, but of many of the top speakers. This was an assembly that celebrated changed lives.

For a moment, Ray wondered if his life was going to change. Would he take the new job? Would he enjoy this type of work? Is travel, living in a hotel and eating out on an expense account, really as bad as he imagined? He wondered what change might be ahead of him.

Reggie arrived early and made his way down near the front. He found his excitement strange, but not uncomfortable. The speakers the night before had kept his attention like nothing he had ever experienced. There was something magical about what was happening.

He sat next to a father and son. He didn't want to eavesdrop, but the proximity made their conversation impossible to ignore. Both were adults, but their interaction was more like what you would expect between friends. Reggie wondered what gave them such a close relationship. He didn't know his own father and had never witnessed a father and son relate like them.

The crowd grew by the minute. Soon his row was packed. Reggie was proud that he had arrived so early and was amazed that he was front and center, only a few rows from the stage.

Seats this close would normally cost a fortune at a concert or other event where you would see these people, he thought. What luck!

Clarke was ready. He had packed everything he

would need in a small bag with a shoulder strap. The bag would remain in the trunk until the appointed time. His plan was a simple assault. There was a door that gave access to what appeared to be an orchestra pit. It also gave a partially obstructed view of the crowd.

He had debated long and hard, trying to decide on the best way to transport his weapon. There were a number of factors to consider, and he had finally made his selection. The paintball gun with hopper and CO2 tank and two extra canisters of paintballs on a duty belt fit perfectly inside the bag. It looked like any oversized gym bag commonly carried around the outdoor basketball courts of any inner-city park.

A handgun he had purchased in a gun-show parking lot was his choice as a backup weapon. It could easily be concealed and only withdrawn if needed. The accuracy at short range was more than adequate. He didn't plan to use it unless he was cornered and needed it for inducing panic rather than injury.

He had memorized the schedule from the program he had picked up the previous evening. The meeting had run slightly behind schedule on Friday, so he was ready if there was some delay. The speaker that had originally drawn his attention was scheduled for 10:45 a.m. The schedule had his name and his claim to fame, "National Outdoor Rifle Champion." That would be followed by a time of worship to be led by a singer Clarke didn't know, and then the biggest name of the morning was scheduled at 11:25. He knew that they would never get to hear the singer; his actions would surely end the program.

The number that had arrived early surprised him. All of the closest parking spaces were already taken. He parked as close as he could and carefully registered the most direct route to and from each visible exit before he got out of his car. He realized that his eco-friendly car was not out of place like it had been at the gun show in Warner Robins. A smile emerged on his face as this rather insignificant fact registered. It was almost soothing, like a bit of comic relief in the midst of a tense movie plot.

Kent's flight into Atlanta arrived on time. He sent a brief text to Ray while the plane was taxiing to the gate to let him know he was on schedule. His overnight bag and briefcase were all he had. Checked bags only caused delays, and he seldom checked luggage anymore.

Helen knew about Kent's plans to meet Ray, but she made her way to the airport to surprise Kent anyway. She waited at the top of the escalators that transported everyone from the last train stop to the terminal baggage claim area. It was the only exit from Atlanta's multiple concourses, and Kent would be forced to exit there regardless.

She had gotten his flight information from Kayla, who was more than happy to be an accomplice in her plan. She had anxiously watched his flight on the arrival screens and had seen it change from "On Time" to "At the Gate."

She began to watch the sporadic flow of arriving passengers. The reception for arriving military personnel was the most obvious and their hugs and kisses were long and fun to watch. Most passengers hurriedly made their way without any fanfare.

Helen waited to surprise Kent. She thought that this would be the start to another special weekend. She had begun to wonder if she might have missed him somehow. It seemed like an eternity before he finally appeared.

He didn't see her at first. He was focused on his objective and walked at a quick pace. Helen began to walk toward him on a collision course. Kent finally noticed her.

She welcomed him with a smile that brought a smile to his face too. There was something special about their relationship.

"What are you doing here?" a hint of delight was in his voice.

"Just here to welcome home a weary traveler. Do you know anyone like that?"

"I don't know. I guess you could say that I'm a weary traveler in need of rescue." He ducked his head slightly and quickly thought of how he might change his plans to meet Ray.

Playfully, she responded, "I guess you'll do." She slipped her arm around his waist and began to walk with him.

"Oh really!" he mocked. "Is this a good place to pick up strangers?"

"I'll have to let you know if I have any luck. Up until now, I haven't seen any of my type."

He decided to break the bad news to her before things went any further. "I have a meeting with a potential team member today and I'm going straight there."

"I know. Kayla knows everything," she was proud of her knowledge and didn't mind showing off.

"So where's your car?" he asked.

"It's at home." She looked him straight in the eyes and continued, "Any idea where I might find a ride?" She raised her eyebrows and waited for a response.

"Well, you might need to work on this pick-up thing you've got going. Usually the person doing the picking up has a vehicle."

"Not if she talked to Kayla. I even know where you usually park your beamer."

"Really?" he responded with a heavy dose of sarcasm.

"Yep, I know just about everything I need to

know."

"Okay, what don't you know?"

"How much time this meeting with the new guy is going to take."

"It just got shortened," he chuckled. "I don't think it will take long at all."

"If you'll let me drive that fancy car of yours," she said, fully into this teasing dialog, "I'll drive to the closest bookstore with a coffee shop and wait impatiently for you to finish."

"We'll see what we can do." He pointed to one of the parking lot vans, "This one will take us to your chariot."

They boarded the van and rode to the parking lot. The driver deposited them at his vehicle and they were on their way in minutes.

Chapter 37

Clarke stood just inside the entrance to the main aisle of the worship center. The entrance was like a short tunnel that is common in many sports stadiums. It was under the front edge of the balcony and with the slope of the floor, the seats on either side made a sheltered area inside the doors. This area was not in the normal view of the crowd. Only those seated forward could actually see back into the recessed area, and it required them to turn around almost completely. He wondered if this was a good place for his plans.

The main worship center was filling up quickly, but that did not matter to Clarke. There were a number of men walking up and down the aisles, so he took a stroll and used it as an opportunity to survey each person seated near the front. He looked at each man and tried to identify any that might try to intervene and spoil his plan. He took extra time with those on the end of each of the front six or seven rows. These would be the closest to what was about to happen and would have the most time to react. Clarke didn't want any heroes.

Ray had gotten out of his truck and was walking the grounds. He was looking for potential security weaknesses in the building and for a while was not focused on the event itself. He had received the text from Kent and knew he was already on his way from the airport.

There were no windows into the main worship center. This would allow the lighting to be managed to optimize the area for video cameras. A church this size had the best video and audio equipment money can buy. The lighting would rival any major TV studio.

Ray finally made his way inside. He enjoyed the first speaker. His presentation had been funny and even made him laugh out loud a few times. In spite of the interesting and humorous delivery, Ray was preoccupied with the decision he faced. It made him uncharacteristically anxious. He had a difficult time sitting still.

As the speaker finished, he got up to move around. He checked his phone for another text from Kent with an update on his arrival, but still no new message. He didn't know that Kent was only a few blocks away and preoccupied with his passenger.

The person on the platform was making announcements. There was a steady flow of men in and out taking advantage of the break.

Ray ended up walking outside and sitting in his

truck. The parking lot was calm. No movement of cars or people.

Ray sat silently, thinking about the pros and cons of the new job. It was his if he wanted it. His own indecisiveness bothered him. At times he wanted to take the job and he felt excited about the team, the work, and most of all, the change. At other times, he was unsure.

Inside, the music ended and someone began to introduce the "National Outdoor Rifle Champion." Clarke had positioned himself in the small tunnel-like hallway and was standing just inside the doors. He took the introduction as his signal. He immediately turned and headed for his car.

A war began to rage in his head as he walked. This was the perfect opportunity. He was ready to strike a blow that would forever change the gun community. He had decided to take what they were fighting for and use it against them. He knew he could still abort. It was not too late to just get in his car and drive away. But he couldn't escape the fact that somebody had to do something. It was now up to him.

He used his key fob to open the trunk a few steps before he reached his vehicle. The trunk lid hovered over the opening. Clarke instinctively looked around as he reached for it. He didn't see a single soul.

He thrust his arm into the trunk to retrieve the bag he had so carefully packed. He hesitated for a fraction of a second, and then reached beyond the bag with the paintball gun to another longer bag. He had instantly changed his plans, right then and there. His thoughts became crystal clear; it was time to show this rifle champion what a rifle can do.

He held the bag at his side in an effort to be as inconspicuous as possible; however, any bag designed to hold a rifle is not easy to disguise. Clarke turned and moved across the parking lot as quickly and smoothly as possible. His focus turned into a type of tunnel vision. He had one objective, and he shut out everything else.

Ray was seated in his truck debating whether to return to the meeting now or later. He expected Kent to arrive any minute. He had seen Clarke walking briskly out of the building and assumed he was leaving. He thought, He's probably late for an appointment.

When Clarke reappeared, his pace was deliberate, but faster than normal. The bag offered little camouflage for its contents. Ray knew immediately that something was terribly wrong. He had surveyed this venue and this event well enough to know that there was nothing out there that would stop this man if he intended to do harm.

He slid out of the cab and reached behind the seat

for the handgun that had made hundreds of commutes with him. Still in its holster, he slipped it into his belt in the center of his back, under his jacket. The man was about to enter the building when Ray began to hurry after him.

Ray knew that his license to carry in Georgia had a specific provision prohibiting anyone, except sworn law enforcement officers, from carrying a weapon into any "house of worship." He didn't think it would matter. His thoughts continued to race, accelerating as he moved.

He knew he had no choice but to follow this guy and see what was up. He would simply investigate this suspicious character and then return the gun to his truck. He really didn't have time to think about everything. In his mind, he was doing what anybody would do if they saw someone carrying what looked like a rifle into a building full of people. Something in his gut told him this was going to lead to tragedy.

Kent pulled into the parking area as Clarke made his final steps across the parking lot. He immediately recognized the long bag. The hurried step of the man turned his suspicion into full alarm.

He quickly pulled to the curb near a side door. He pointed out the suspicious man and asked Helen if she had her gun with her. His actions were crisp

Unforeseen Impact 225

and deliberate.

"Quick, hand me your gun. I don't carry mine when I fly."

She retrieved her weapon and handed it to Kent. "It is loaded just like you taught me."

"Call 911 and tell them that there is a suspicious man with what appears to be a rifle. Tell them that armed plainclothes security are also on the scene."

He jumped out of the car and began to run toward the door. He chambered a round, released the hammer, and checked the magazine as he ran. Just before he reached the door, he slipped the pistol into his pocket.

Everything was happening quickly now. As Ray entered the door, he caught a glimpse of Clarke as he disappeared into the main hall. Ray moved quickly and began to jog.

Clarke paused once he was inside the door. He pulled the rifle from its case and dropped the bag on the ground. His mind was racing. Adrenaline was coursing through his body. He felt as if everyone in the room could hear his heart beating. He was still in the short tunnel-like area, with the gun down at his side close to the wall. No one had seen the weapon. He looked down at the rifle and flipped off the safety. He took his first step forward and the second came easier.

Ray looked through the peephole designed for the ushers to use. He could see Clark had already begun to walk forward with the rifle at his side. Ray reached for the gun in his belt and slid inside the door.

Kent was entering a side door near the front as Clarke began to walk down the aisle. The rifle was still at Clarke's side as Kent moved to the edge of the tunnel. Kent had his hand on the pistol and he flicked off the safety and pulled the hammer into position as he drew it from his coat pocket and held it down by his side.

Kent surveyed his options. The slope of floor placed the crowd directly behind Clarke as he made his way down the aisle. Kent didn't have a clear shot without putting others in the direct line of fire. He began to consider other options. His last resort would be to rush the shooter and use surprise to his advantage.

Al was in the sound booth and had a clear line of sight of the entire worship center. The tragedy unfolded right before his eyes, and he was frozen in horror. He could never have imagined a gunman walking down the aisle toward the platform right in the middle of a packed event.

Ray disengaged the safety and cocked the hammer as he brought his gun around his body. He crouched down as he opened the door and slipped into the relative darkness of the corridor.

Ray wanted to yell to distract the shooter, but there

was noise coming from all around him as the crowd began to register that this individual was armed with a high-powered rifle.

Clarke raised the rifle as he neared the front. He looked through the scope and tried to locate his target. He had prepared a one-line speech to deliver before he fired, but it was lost in the excitement of the moment.

Kent drew his weapon, but still could not safely fire from his vantage point. The options were quickly running out. He prepared to respond with the only option he had left; he would charge the gunman. The distance was too far, but there weren't any other options. He knew that the gunman would have plenty of time to react and turn his gun on him.

Ray was on one knee with his pistol raised when he heard the deafening sound of the rifle. He aimed and fired two quick shots. The second bullet didn't matter, because the first hit its mark almost perfectly. The police investigation would find the second round lodged in the wall behind the platform.

Clarke never knew what hit him. His last thought as he aimed again for a second shot was, How did I miss him? Ray's first round hit Clarke in the temple before Clarke could get off a second shot. The bullet ended his life with a merciful quickness. His head jerked with the impact and his body slumped to the floor. The rifle tumbled to the ground harmlessly.

Ray was stunned. It had all happened in a matter of seconds. He moved from his knee and sat on the floor and leaned against the wall. The terror that he had been too late to stop the first killing was all he could think about. The crowd rushed by, but he sat motionless against the wall.

He did not yet know that Clarke had missed and that the round had not done any damage to life or limb. Due to his inexperience, Clarke had made a simple mistake. He tried to locate a target in his scope that was too close. The bullet from Clark's first shot had simply lodged in the wall after shattering a light.

Reggie had seen the scenario unfolding only a few yards away. He heard the crowd begin to react and first saw the gunman out of the corner of his eye. He watched as the man raised his rifle. The boom of the rifle and then the sound of two more shots reverberated across the room. His eyes were fixed on Clarke when the bullet penetrated his temple. It was evident that death came instantaneously.

The event jerked him back in time. The muzzle flash replayed in his mind and the images of a dying man were inescapable. This was different, but the haunting memories came pouring back and were impossible to turn off.

He made his way close enough to see the lifeless body lying on the carpet. Blood had oozed out and puddled under the gunman's head. Lifelessness gave the appearance of peacefulness. To Reggie, another death by a gun only increased his pain. The inner struggle raged, and absolution evaded him at every turn.

Reggie was filled with horror and wondered if he would ever know peace again. Part of him wanted to confess and tell someone what he had done. Fear kept him quiet. Guilt bore a hole in him that felt like a massive gash in his soul. He wanted peace, but he felt more like a victim than ever before.

Kent approached Ray and sat down beside him. They sat in silence for a while. Kent placed his hand on Ray's shoulder and quietly said, "I saw the whole thing. You did the right thing today."

They sat there without moving until the police arrived.

Helen called Kent's cell phone and he answered before the second ring. "I'm fine."

"Where are you?" the fear was obvious in her voice.

"I'm near the back, but I'll meet you at the door where you saw me go in."

Kent moved quickly to the exit and found Helen. They shared a long embrace.

"What happened?"

He gave an abbreviated account of the events. He ended with a simple summary, "The gunman is dead, and I never had to fire your gun."

Helen leaned into his chest and lingered there a long time. Her mind raced as she tried to comprehend what had just happened. She was glad Kent was there. She wondered if she could have shot the gunman.

The police and other first responders went to work. Ray was identified as the man who had stopped the shooter. He was questioned by several police officers, and his gun was taken as evidence. Detectives also interviewed him and took formal statements.

Al was thrust in the middle of all that was happening. Busyness and activity were a welcome distraction. They were an odd diversion, but he needed them to cope with what had just happened before his eyes. Time would come soon enough when he would evaluate every detail. For now, he was glad that only one life was lost. He was thankful for someone who broke the rules and brought a gun into his "house of worship." He knew better than anyone that this could have been much worse.

Hours had passed by the time Ray was allowed to leave. He had been stoically calm throughout the investigation process. He played the scene over and over again in his thoughts. The fact that he had taken the life of another person weighed heavy on his mind. He questioned his judgment. He questioned himself. Everyone was glad the shooter was dead, but he was the one who had pulled the trigger. Many had assured him he had done the right thing, but he couldn't escape the truth—he had killed a man.

Chapter 38

As Ray walked toward his pickup he was amazed at the array of news agencies that lined the curb. Each van or truck was equipped for remote broadcast.

Reporters and their crews jockeyed for position as they reported via live feeds and prerecorded spots. The background for these shots was important to the cameramen as well as the reporters. They both wanted their viewers to know that they were broadcasting live, directly from the scene. The cameramen generally just did as they were told, but a few insisted on some type of creative cinematic effect.

Jennifer and her crew had been some of the first to arrive and had staked out one of the best locations. Boredom was a gentle motivator during the long wait between live broadcasts, and her cameraman had worked out how to zoom the camera from a wide shot of the church building, with the reporter in the foreground, to a close-up of the reporter with the building still visible in the background. He had employed his camera magic on several of the live "breaking news" reports they had broadcast.

This tragic event provided national coverage, and Jennifer recognized the importance of the broader exposure. She wouldn't let this tragedy go to waste.

She wished she had dressed differently, but it was far too late to do anything about it. She consoled herself with the thought that her appearance somehow bestowed a degree of authenticity to the report.

One benefit of working for the local network news was the easy access she had to the major news wires. She knew how to leverage information that others in the field had gathered. The airways and news wires were quickly flooded on major news stories, and someone had to filter through them to separate fact from conjecture. Those in the field were often in the best position to verify the rapidly emerging information. There was no need to carve out a niche for the local audience; the broader exposure was the priority. If a local connection existed, it might be woven into the local broadcast, but the real priorities were speed and accuracy.

Jennifer had worked hard to be ready for each broadcast. She had fine-tuned her reports to include the facts as they were unearthed. What really happened? Who was involved? and How many were killed and injured? These were the questions on everyone's mind. Yet, the simple facts are not always easy to ascertain. In the rush to be first, accuracy often takes a backseat in these "breaking news" events.

Hours had slowly passed since the shots were fired. As day turned to darkness, the information rush had given way to increased accuracy and a focus of details.

The final police statement for the evening was carried live by many of the news networks and recorded by all. Clarke's name was not officially released. Reporters already knew much about him and had been adding details about him all afternoon and evening as they were discovered. The police spokesperson introduced himself and read a carefully worded statement.

"I am Lieutenant Espinosa and I will provide copies of the statement I am about to read to members of the press.

"At approximately 10:51 a.m., a lone gunman entered the church with a high powered rifle. The venue was approximately ninety-five percent filled to capacity at the time of the incident with an estimated attendance of more than 2,300 individuals.

"Three minutes after he entered the building with the rifle, the gunman discharged his weapon in the direction of the event speaker. He fired only one shot. The round did not strike anyone, and he was fatally shot before he could make any additional attempts.

"The perpetrator's name is being withheld,

pending further investigation and the notification of next of kin. This is an ongoing investigation and we are not at liberty to provide additional information about this individual at this time.

"A civilian, Mr. Ray Williams, of Ellijay, Georgia, observed the events unfolding and retrieved a weapon from his vehicle. Following the initial shot fired by the perpetrator, Mr. Williams intervened. He fired two rounds and fatally wounded the gunman.

"Mr. Williams has cooperated fully with the investigation. He is licensed to carry a concealed handgun, and his actions prevented the gunman from killing and/or injuring others. Mr. Williams' actions are considered justified, and he will not be charged.

"We anticipate that we will be able to provide additional information at our next scheduled briefing, tomorrow at nine a.m."

Lieutenant Espinosa added his own observation to the written statement: "Mr. Williams should be considered a hero for his actions today." Then he offered to take a few questions.

Jennifer listened for confirmation of what she had heard, "a gunshot to the head." She had heard it from another reporter and the images from her past had come roaring back. She avoided the body of the dead gunman. It would be covered anyway, she told herself. But fear of her own demons had kept her far away.

She wanted to ask at least one sharp gun-control-related question. She saw her chance to get her voice and her clearly stated opposition on every network, yet the flood of images in her memory paralyzed her. She felt like a victim once again. The lifeless body of the teenager, the blood that seemed to cover everything that fateful night, the horror of the scene dominated every thought. She was never able to ask a question.

As the police spokesman stepped away from the microphones, she overheard another reporter say, "He was stopped by a fatal gunshot to the head." The words awakened feelings and emotions that she thought had been laid to rest long ago. She wondered if Mr. Williams would be haunted by images and emotions from this day.

Chapter 39

The next day was Sunday and Ray went to church with his wife. He was greeted as a hero. It seemed everyone had heard what had happened, and they were proud of him. They were thrilled that they knew this hero personally. There was a lot of backslapping and everyone wanted to shake his hand.

Monday would have been a workday like any other, except Ray went into the office as a hero. He received the same treatment he had gotten at church the day before.

What they didn't see was the inner struggle that Ray hid from everyone. They would never understand. Ray would not have understood before 10:54 a.m. the day before. Ray had replayed the sight of the impact over and over in his mind. He couldn't escape it. It haunted him. He had taken a man's life with his gun and nothing would ever change that fact.

Ray had seen a seeming endless flood of news reports about his actions. Yet, somehow he was still drawn to watch. Weeks had passed and every detail of his actions had been dissected and analyzed. Tonight's broadcast was more of the same. The talking heads were presenting opposing views.

"Mr. Williams is a hero. His actions prevented a much greater loss of life. We need more people like him, willing to get involved," stated one of the TV news guests.

The retort by another was sharp, "He was nothing more than a vigilante, a self-appointed judge, jury and executioner. If everyone takes matters into their own hands, we'll have gunslingers everywhere."

Another jumped in, "He broke the law. He carried his weapon into a 'house of worship.' Lawlessness, that's all this was. The supporters of the Second Amendment want to take this nation back to the Wild West."

"Lawlessness already exists in many of our cities," came a gentle reply. "It is not the law-abiding gun owners who are escalating the murder rates. Guns are not the cause."

The debate droned on. Ray bristled at the harsh tone and felt a sharp sting from some of the painful rhetoric. His emotions covered the gamut. Pundits had ranged from affirmation to condemnation. Some had contempt for his actions, while others saw a hero.

In the weeks, months and even years ahead, Ray's actions would be affirmed and cheered. They would also be questioned and condemned.

Gun control advocates would use Clarke as an example of the evil that lurks in the world of gun ownership. They would label Ray an executioner. They would argue that he was not licensed to carry his firearm in a "house of worship." They would use the bloody images as weapons in their war against guns and their fight for gun control.

Advocates of gun ownership would use Ray as an example of why the Second Amendment must be defended. They would use this event to demonstrate the protection that we enjoy when responsible people are properly armed. The events, especially the fact that no one but the shooter was killed or even injured, would become ammunition for the war they would wage.

This clash of beliefs about what is right and what is wrong was not changed by the shots fired that fateful Saturday. Ray simply felt like a pawn in their game.

He observed that a war of words erupted with each news story involving guns. The locations changed and the casualties had different names, just like battles in any war, but the war continued. The war over guns and gun ownership would continue to be waged.

Chapter 40

Ray decided he needed a change. He took the offer from Bree Security Consultants and started a new career. He enjoyed the travel for a while, but it quickly grew old. He couldn't bring himself to sell his house and land. So, he endured the long commute on the days he had to be in the office, but loved the days he worked from home.

He became very creative about working from home and was now pushing Kent to close the office. "I love technology," had become his mantra. "I can attend a meeting from my house, and it is just like being there." Kent was finding his arguments increasingly difficult to dismiss.

Ray's life had changed. He was now a security consultant and that was more positive than negative. Perhaps it helped that several of his fellow consultants had military backgrounds. The only real clue came from Kent. He once made a private comment to Ray, "You're not the only member of this team that has had to take another man's life." There was no explanation, and Ray didn't need one.

The part that changed Ray the most was one simple fact; he had taken another man's life with a gun. Any kind of gun never again felt the same in his hands.